T0279427

THE MEMORY MONSTER

"A brilliant short novel that serves as a brave, sharp-toothed brief against letting the past devour the present. . . . Other writers have described well the reverberations of trauma (like David Grossman in *See Under: Love*) but few have taken this further step, to wonder out loud about the ways the Holocaust may have warped the collective conscience of a nation, making every moment existential, a constant panic not to become victims again."

GAL BECKERMAN, *NEW YORK TIMES
BOOK REVIEW*, EDITORS' CHOICE

"Award-winning Israeli novelist Sarid's latest work is a slim but powerful novel, rendered beautifully in English by translator Greenspan. . . . Propelled by the narrator's distinctive voice, the novel is an original variation on one of the most essential themes of post-Holocaust literature: While countless writers have asked the question of where, or if, humanity can be found within the profoundly inhumane, Sarid incisively shows how preoccupation and obsession with the inhumane can take a toll on one's own humanity. . . . it is, if not an indictment of Holocaust memorialization, a nuanced and trenchant consideration of its layered politics. Ultimately, Sarid both refuses to apologize for Jewish rage and condemns the nefarious forms it sometimes takes. A bold, masterful exploration of the banality of evil and the nature of revenge, controversial no matter how it is read."

KIRKUS REVIEWS, STARRED REVIEW

"A brilliant, challenging, and uncompromising novel. . . . It lays bare the hard truth, often obscured by a too-hopeful vision of humanity, that Holocaust education has not led to a softer, kinder world, and 'Never Again' merely means 'never again for us.'"

MITCHELL ABIDOR, JEWISH CURRENTS

"Award-winning Yishai Sarid's slender, elegantly translated novel grapples with some mighty questions, among them the myriad ways in which the Holocaust might be seen to have shaped Israel's culture, and the complex existential politics of memorialisation and Holocaust education. . . . Where the book excels is in its readiness to court controversy without surrendering nuance, and in place of moralising it offers questioning that's as necessary as it is unsettling."

HEPHZIBAH ANDERSON, GUARDIAN

"*The Memory Monster* is one of the great Israeli novels to have been published in translation in recent years. Sarid's book is wonderfully subversive, darkly humorous; riveting, challenging, and thought-provoking. The voice—captured well in English by Yardenne Greenspan—is finely balanced, teetering on the edge as the memory monster sinks its teeth deeper and deeper into Sarid's protagonist. *The Memory Monster* is a novel that demands to be read and deserves our attention."

LIAM HOARE, FATHOM

"[A] record of a breakdown, an impassioned consideration of memory and its risks, and a critique of Israel's use of the Holocaust to shape national identity. . . . Sarid's unrelenting examination of how narratives of the Holocaust are shaped makes for much more than the average confessional tale."

"Sarid's incisive critique of Holocaust memorialization, the corruption within it, and the perverse forms of nationalism it can engender is courageous. . . . It unabashedly critiques the link between Holocaust remembrance culture and the tendency of certain strains of Jewish and particularly Israeli culture to overrate the centrality of aggressive survivorship to Jewish identity, and how this culture in turn nurtures the militarization, settler colonialism, and Islamophobia that combine to create the perfect storm of violent right-wing nationalism. . . . Nuanced and subtle at every level."

MIRANDA COOPER, *LOS ANGELES REVIEW OF BOOKS*

"*The Memory Monster* is shattering, brilliant, disturbing, and very important. Sarid's background as a lawyer makes the narrator's arguments—and his falling apart—all the more disturbing when his logic fails. How can the horrors of the Holocaust be taught, remembered? A powerful novel."

LYNNE TILLMAN, AUTHOR OF *MEN AND APPARITIONS*

"The short, but powerful novel raises the question of how far we let the horrors of the past infiltrate our present day lives. . . . *The Memory Monster* is not an easy book to read but its message is important to hear."

ELLIS SHUMAN, *TIMES OF ISRAEL*

The Investigation of Captain Erez

Limassol

Naomi's Kindergarten

The Third

The Memory Monster

VICTORIOUS

YISHAI SARID

VICTORIOUS

A NOVEL

Translated from the Hebrew by
Yardenne Greenspan

RESTLESS BOOKS
BROOKLYN, NEW YORK

Copyright © 2020 Yishai Sarid
Translation copyright © 2022 Yardenne Greenspan

First published as *Menatzahat* by Am Oved, Tel Aviv, 2020

Published by arrangement with the Institute of the Translation of Hebrew Literature

First Restless Books hardcover edition September 2022

Hardcover ISBN: 9781632063120
Library of Congress Control Number: 2022935833

"And to every people after their language" Book of Esther I .22

Published with the support of the Institute for the Translation of Hebrew Literature, the Consulate General of Israel in New York.

This work is published with support from David Bruce Smith, Grateful American Foundation.

This book is supported in part by an award from the National Endowment for the Arts.

This book is made possible by the New York State Council on the Arts with the support of Governor Kathy Hochul and the New York State Legislature.

Cover design by Daniel Benneworth-Gray
Set in Garibaldi by Tetragon, London
Printed in the United States of America

1 3 5 7 9 10 8 6 4 2

Restless Books, Inc.
232 3rd Street, Suite A101
Brooklyn, NY 11215

www.restlessbooks.org
publisher@restlessbooks.org

"*The dagger wants to kill, it wants to shed sudden blood.*"

JORGE LUIS BORGES, *FICCIONES*

TRANSLATED BY RUTHVEN TODD, HENRY REED, AND HELEN TEMPLE

VICTORIOUS

1

HE'LL SUMMON ME eventually, when the celebrations are over. Wait ten days, two weeks at the most, I told myself. He will call. I watched his inauguration ceremony on the news, with the honorary guard, the assigning of the ranks, and the military band. He could have sent me an invitation, I thought, but I understood why he didn't.

The summons from his office came after two weeks and two days. "The Chief of Staff wants to see you."

"Of course," I said. When Rosolio asks me to come, I come.

My entry permit had expired and the guards at the gate held me up for a long time. I showed them my ID, which stated I was a lieutenant colonel in reserve duty, but they insisted on following proper procedure. I finally made it into his office, a little sweaty and not as fresh as I'd have liked, but right on time. I was never late, anywhere.

"Just a moment," his head of office said. I didn't like the jealous look she gave me. "Please, have a seat," she said, pointing at the waiting area.

After way too long, a group of potbellied men in powder-blue civilian button-downs walked out of his office, and she finally deigned to announce my arrival.

A few seconds later, Rosolio appeared in the doorway, wearing the military's highest insignia. He was as stunning as ever. "Abigail," he said.

"Sir," I answered—it just fell out of my mouth, like I was an idiot—and beamed my biggest smile. I felt immense pride in him, as if he were my older brother, or my man.

The first time I met him, twenty-five years earlier, during one of his battalion's drills in the Golan Heights, I knew he'd make it all the way to the top if he managed not to get killed on the way. He had made it to this office in one piece, though it took him longer than I'd expected. The old images submerged me. I was touched. His body had thickened, but his pleasant scent had remained, as had the hint of masculine flesh hidden behind the uniform and the brass, and his eyes still contained that wise gaze that attracted me more than any physical quality. He was glad I'd come. "Come on in, Abigail," he invited me with a wide gesture, then took a seat behind the desk at

4

which fates were sealed. On the desk was a framed photo of his wife and daughters, which he hadn't bothered to hide for my sake.

"How are you?" I asked. I noticed stress in his tired eyes and slumped head and shoulders, as well as his bitten nails.

"Well, you're looking at it," he chuckled. "Lots of work to do, lots of things to change." The way he spoke was always a little wooden, and I had to chip through it to find the droplets of emotion. A famous topographical map of the Middle East was hanging over his head. He looked lonely. I wanted to go sit next to him, to touch him, massage his stiff shoulder blades, but I wasn't sure how he'd react.

"I've been working like mad," he said. "It's an immense responsibility. You don't realize just how immense until you get here."

I asked what he'd been eating and how much sleep he'd been getting. Over the years, I'd seen Rosolio under all sorts of pressures, and I knew he was strong but not made of iron. He wasn't one of those rare superhumans that the military produces once every generation or two. Now and then, the night before embarking on a military operation or making a crucial decision, he had an intense need for me to hold his hand, offer words of support, reassure him he'd made the right choice, save him from the doubt and confusion and fear involved in sacrificing human life. Rosolio was brave, serious, and smart, but occasionally he became blocked by hesitation and had to be rescued so he could move forward.

I'd gotten dolled up for him, wearing barely perceptible lipstick and a young, spring-scented perfume. My greatest fear was that I'd look old to him, that my body would repulse him. But I could tell by looking into his eyes that I had yet to cross that terrible threshold. He still liked me.

He asked what life as a civilian was like. I told him I hadn't been able to let go, and that I mostly treated veterans suffering from shell shock; that I'd made myself a reputation as someone who specialized in that particular kind of rehabilitation. I told him I still gave talks at Command and Staff, and that occasionally I did a few days of reserve duty to assist with special missions. "I treated some regular people," I told Rosolio, "but I didn't have patience for them. Their little problems bored me. I sat across from them and couldn't stop yawning."

"Thank God we're helping you make a living," Rosolio joked, then turned serious, as if afraid someone might be watching him through the wall. "We've screwed lots of boys' lives," he said, adding, "and it wasn't always worth it."

"That's not something you ought to be thinking about right now," I told him. "Save that thought for retirement, when you write your memoir."

"Welcome back, Abigail," he laughed. "I've missed you. It's been a long time since anyone gave me some clear instructions on what to think. We're back in the good old days."

Underneath every word we spoke were the things we couldn't say. We were in the Chief of Staff's chambers, the map of the Middle East watching over us, no chance for intimacy. Rosolio scratched the back of his neck and said, "I asked you here today because I think you might be able to help. You always made a special contribution to the force. You didn't just help those who stayed behind, you also helped us stride ahead. That's what I want to do with this entire military. Stride ahead."

Could you be any more formal? I thought. But I said, "Sure, I'm totally in. How can I help?"

"We're fantastic in the air and in the sea," he said. "Fast, efficient, invincible. On land is where we get bogged down, in face-to-face combat. That's where we get killed or abducted. That's where we sink into the mud. These are gentle kids; we never taught them how to kill."

Now I was finally able to frame this meeting: he had asked me here as an expert on the psychology of killing. I crossed my legs, sat up straight. My hair was in a bun, as usual. I said, "Anything they can operate from a distance with the touch of a button comes naturally to them. Killing from afar is no problem. It's like a game. But hurting people up close is a whole other story. These kids barely play out in the yard. They don't even get into fights. Instead of playing with the other neighborhood kids, they text them. Everything is symbolic, the real world barely exists. Sometimes I think we should have taught them to slaughter a chicken or break someone's nose before expecting them to go off and kill other human beings."

Rosolio laughed and said, "Can you imagine what the papers would say if I introduced chicken slaughter into the training program?"

"They don't fuck anymore, either," I said. "They don't even touch each other."

"I only have daughters," Rosolio said, then paused awkwardly and corrected himself. "We only have daughters, so that doesn't bother me as much."

Twenty-five years ago, outside of his battalion commander tent, Rosolio had made me Turkish coffee and we'd shared our views about man as a killing machine. He was eager to talk to me, even though I was just a young academic officer who hadn't encountered a battlefield in her life. I was so flattered.

I wanted to deepen the conversation now too, to impress him, to tell him about new studies conducted by military psychologists in other countries, to boast my knowledge, to demonstrate my professional authority. But his office manager knocked on the door, apologized, and said Rosolio had to head out to a meeting with the minister. They were waiting for him, she emphasized, shooting me a suspicious glance.

"One minute," he said, then waited for her to leave. "How's the kid?" he asked softly, almost whispering. I didn't know if his office was tapped. I decided to proceed with caution.

"His enlistment is in a few days," I reported. I wouldn't have brought it up had he not asked. That deviated from the rules of our agreement.

"Already? What unit?" he asked, surprised, even embarrassed. He had no idea how old Shauli was.

I looked him straight in the eyes and said, "Paratroopers, like you."

"Paratroopers? How come? How did that happen?"

"I've been asking myself the same thing. I must have done a bad job raising him. He could have joined the

Intelligence Corps. He's got a great mind. He could have been a pilot, if he had insisted on being a hero, or a naval officer. He's at the beach all the time, anyway. But no, he wanted to be a paratrooper. An old-fashioned boy. The only one out of all of his friends. He wants to be a man's man. That old shtick still works on him."

"It can't be a coincidence. Did you tell him anything about me? Did you insinuate anything?" Rosolio asked suspiciously.

"No." I made a face. I didn't like that question. I never told and I never would. I'd given Rosolio my word. We had an agreement.

"I'm sorry, Abigail. Of course you didn't," he said softly, appeasing me. I recalled his languidness as he rose from our lovemaking bed, how tenderly he'd treated me. He's one of the good guys, Rosolio. I hadn't been wrong in choosing him. "So he's a big boy now," Rosolio concluded tritely, then glanced at his watch, seeing he was late. "Strange. I probably wouldn't recognize him on the street." He kept saying "him" or "the kid." Rosolio never called Shauli by his name. But that was my fault. I had forbidden any contact between them and never told my son who his father was.

"Come look," I said. Suddenly I felt sorry for both of them and searched for my phone to show him a picture of Shauli. I wanted him to see how tall and handsome our son was. But then I remembered the guards had taken my phone. Too bad. Or maybe it was for the best.

"Paratrooper basic training?" Rosolio suddenly said, his tone amused. "I'll ask around about him."

I tensed. "Don't you dare look for him or ask about him. This is a delicate situation and he's a smart boy. What would he think when the Chief of Staff suddenly asks about him? He knows you used to be my commander. He'll put two and two together."

"You're right, I'll keep my mouth shut," Rosolio said, twisting the doorknob, ready to rush off to his meeting with the minister.

"Hang on," I said. I stood up in front of him and took hold of his epauletted shoulders. I wanted to empower him and had to resist the urge to hug him. "Get me back in here when you're ready. I want to stride ahead with you."

He leaned in for a flash, then pushed out of the room.

2

I DROVE SHAULI to the recruitment center along with a few of his closest friends. We waited for his name to appear on the screen, a sign it was his turn to get on the bus. I tried to hold on to memories of his childhood—birthdays, kindergarten celebrations, parent-teacher conferences, countless meals enjoyed together, just the two of us. But all the years that had gone by now collapsed on my head like an avalanche, leaving nothing behind. I rubbed his shoulders, held his hand, reminded him over and over not to hesitate to call me with any problem, because I knew people in the military.

Shauli told me not to worry; he was sure he'd be all right. He joked around with his friends, and for some reason I thought about a bride traveling alone across the continent, something I'd once seen in an old movie. His friends loved him, worried about him, and were surprised by him, because none of them even considered volunteering for combat service. They no longer needed this challenge to confirm their masculinity. But I was proud to have made him this way all on my own, open and kind, and was worried about what might happen to him on the other side, when I handed him over to the military. One of the walls boasted a large portrait of Rosolio along with the Chief of Staff's well wishes to new recruits. I almost said, *Look, that's your father on the wall. He'll keep you safe. He'll run into the fire with you.* Instead I told myself, This is your fault. Shauli studied your eyes, your voice, and the frequency of the air around you and figured out which men you respect and which you don't, and he realized the brave and tough guys were the only ones you were willing to tolerate, and sensed how much distaste you have for the softer ones.

During his final days as a civilian, Shauli went out surfing, his skin growing tan in the sun. In the evenings, he played basketball in the schoolyard, and at night his friends filled our apartment. I served them soda and fruit and ordered them pizza. Some of them stayed over, crowding the floor of his bedroom. It was a long and raucous goodbye. They held on to each other until he had to go.

Now I ran my hand through his hair and told him he should have cut it. I was restless.

He said, "Mom, you're much more nervous than I am, and you spent so many years in the military. Is there something you aren't telling me about what goes on there?"

I winced. "No, no, everything's going to be just fine, I'm just having trouble saying goodbye." This wasn't the right time to discuss the deeper issues. Then his name and ID number appeared on the screen, and the loud-speaker urged new recruits to board the bus. We walked him to the turnstile, his friends sprayed water on him from a plastic bottle, and when he got on the bus he waved at us through the window.

When I got home, I tidied his bedroom from the chaos of the last few days, so it would be ready for him when he came home on leave. Before slipping his guitar back into its case, I tried strumming a few chords, but I couldn't play, and no real tune came out. You're just nervous, I told myself. He'll be home next Saturday, or the one after that, and his friends will come over, and three years will pass this way, after which he'll embark on the wonderful life he deserves.

*

I told Mandy I was by myself now. He came to visit and brought me a gift: a little iron figurine he'd made of a woman looking up at the sky, her body twisted like a distorted Canaanite goddess.

"Is that me?" I asked.

He growled his bearish laugh.

He'd come a long way, all the way from his village, and asked permission to stay the night. In addition to the figurine, he brought a can of olive oil from his grove. I used the oil to cook us omelets and chopped some salad. I told Mandy I wasn't used to this quiet, that the apartment felt too empty, that I missed Shauli and couldn't stop wondering how he was doing.

"Come live with me," he said. "I'm lonely too."

Then we sat on the balcony and watched the street, the illuminated apartments and the figures walking through them as if upon a stage at a shadow-puppet show. I touched the scars on his hand, my fingers attempting to distinguish the ones left from injuries caused by his sharp crafting tools, the ones made by working the land, and from the other, older ones, caused by that long-ago time in his life that had led to our acquaintance.

Mandy was the only person I'd persuaded to come to therapy. I read a newspaper interview with him, published in light of a retrospective held in his honor at the Tel Aviv Museum of Art. He spoke about his shell shock, the screaming in the night, and the violent visions he experienced during the day. I calculated and figured he was about fifteen years older than I. The reporter wrote that no new pieces were being shown at the exhibition because Mandy hadn't been able to make any art in recent years. I went to the museum and was deeply touched by his work. He created difficult, violent sculptures that stood out in the gallery, lonesome and vicious, appearing to be on the verge of breaking.

I mustered my courage and called him. I told him I loved his art, that I'd read the newspaper piece about him, and that I thought I might be able to help him get back into art making.

"Come see me and we'll talk," he said.

He lived in the countryside, on the edge of a nearly deserted immigrant village, across from a rocky cliff planted with pine trees. His property included a fecund orchard where crows pecked at pomegranates and shoved their heads into the red pulp as if gnawing at human skulls.

"We used to have lots of fruit here," he apologized, "but then my wife died and I ran out of steam. I let my mind take over, and it shows me whatever it wants. Evil, upsetting images that I can't do anything about."

He took me to his olive grove and told me that he used to be able to produce two hundred and sixty gallons a year but that recently he couldn't be bothered. His artwork had also turned into meaningless lumps of raw material.

"I'm tapped out," he said. "I don't have a drop of moisture left."

I looked at his wrinkled face, his strong shoulders, and knew I'd be able to revive him. There was enough energy in there for me to work with. He took me to his workshop, filled with ironsmithing tools, and showed me all his halfway finished, abandoned sculptures. "There's nothing there," he said, "just pieces of soulless iron."

"The soul will return." I smiled at him. I was impressed with his studio, and no less so by the fact that he'd invited me in.

Then we sat in his house, where Mandy brewed tea from herbs he grew in the garden. "I don't know why I let you come here," he said. "I was going to cancel. But I'm glad you came. You don't nag, and I like talking to you."

A strong wind blew outside and there was no one around, as if the entire village were deserted. Mandy peeled an orange, handing me one section at a time, and told me about the people he'd killed a long time ago, who were now returning to take revenge, ruining his life. His hand gestures told the whole story. How he'd killed by stabbing, strangling, shooting, always silently and at point blank.

"Imagine meeting someone for the first time," he said, "and immediately moving close enough to him to smell him, to hear his breath, to read his expression, and within a second or two you penetrate his body with a knife or a bullet. You're with him in his final moments. Not his wife, not his parents, not his kids. You're the only one there. Sometimes they fell into my arms and mumbled parting words. There was nobody else."

"It sounds like they only started bothering you in the past few years," I said.

"True," said Mandy. "Until now I've managed to keep them at a distance. They didn't dare come near. I killed them a second time in my memory. But after my wife died they started coming and I couldn't stop them. They must have sensed I was weak. They insist on speaking to me, showing me their wounds, taking me back to that final moment, and then I choke. I can't breathe and everything around me dies."

It got dark outside, and Mandy told me about one of the people that haunted his nights, a high-ranking commander of a terrorist faction. Mandy's force had sailed overseas to assassinate him. When our soldiers quietly infiltrated his house, they found him in the bathroom, wearing pajamas, putting drops in his eyes. They grabbed his wife in the living room and injected her with tranquilizer. In his dream, the man kept telling him, "Just wait until I finish putting in the drops, it's rude to just barge in like this," but Mandy couldn't wait and had to shoot him in the head with a silenced gun. In his dreams he was very preoccupied with the eye drops. The man's eyes were red, as if he'd spent too much time reading or out in the sun, but it didn't matter—he was going to die. And still the man insisted, walking closer to Mandy, who was having trouble squeezing the trigger, which is a difficulty he'd never encountered in waking life.

"What did you used to do when you were younger?" I asked. "How'd you get rid of these apparitions?"

Mandy explained that he would spot them from afar and go out drinking, smoking, meeting a new girl, delving into work on a new sculpture, and that kept them away. "But now they won't leave me alone," he said, "they just sit here in my brain."

I convinced him to come into the city for therapy. It was a success. He had strong mental resources and creative force, thanks to which we were able to push the trauma back into hiding. Occasionally the people he killed managed to sneak in through nightmares.

I wasn't able to block their nocturnal visits completely, but he regained full functionality in the daytime. When I announced that our therapy sessions were over, Mandy invited me to visit him again.

I came for a day visit in the spring and ended up staying nearly a week. I didn't want to leave. We restored his orchard together, I watched him as he worked on his twisted, wounded, sublime figures in his studio. He let me get very close to him, as if my presence shooed away bad memories. He wanted me to stay there for good, and I thought to myself: like a living scarecrow. I was attracted to him, I respected him, I envied his talent, but I couldn't stay there. I promised to come visit often.

3

I CALLED DAD to see if he needed me to get any groceries for him. Dad said groceries were no problem, the store delivered them, but it would be great if I could get him some fruit at the greengrocers. Shauli used to bring over fruit once a week, and now that he'd enlisted I had to fill in for him. Shauli loved going to my father's. At the end of every visit, Dad would give him two hundred shekels. But he didn't go there for the money. Dad was tender and sensitive with him, offering him all the love he'd deprived me of. I don't like visiting him because it's hard for me to resist him. He'd hardly left the house since Mom died, and he was having trouble walking. Once again, I offered to get him a live-in caretaker, but he was stubborn. He cooked for himself and washed his own clothes, and the only help he was willing to accept was a maid who came once a week. Dad was eighty-four years old, and the cancer in his blood platelets was slowly stealing away his life.

A few days later, when I had a free afternoon, I was startled to recall his request and rushed off to the greengrocers to buy him some expensive, great-looking fruit. I delivered them to him without prior notice—he lived just a few blocks away from me. As soon as I opened the door I could sense the cramped presence of a patient. My footsteps turned soft at once; I should have called first. I saw the closed sliding door in the living room, confirmation that he was in his clinic with a patient. I silently placed the bags in the kitchen and held my ear against the wall. All I could pick up were muffled voices. I tiptoed to the living room and sat down on the sofa. That's how silent Mom and I would become whenever he had a patient, making ourselves disappear lest any part of the psychoanalyst's real, normal life be revealed, reducing the realm of fantasy that was so crucial for treatment. What would happen if I slid open the door, poked my head in just for a moment, and said, *Hey Dad, sorry for the interruption, I brought you some fruit, see you later*, then took off? I would never be brave enough to do that, I admitted to myself.

I knew Dad still saw a few of his longtime patients, to whom he presented a strong front. He greeted them in the door with quiet formality, saying, "Please, come in," then followed them into the clinic at the edge of the hall, separated from the rest of the apartment by a squeaky sliding door. His clinic contained a classic sofa for the patient to lie on, a comfy armchair for Dad, a thick Persian rug, and a naive painting of the Jerusalem Mountains, gifted to him by an important artist he once treated. When I was a kid, his clinic seemed like the most mysterious, most important place on earth. That was where he used words to get into people's brains, see their problems, and care for them so that they weren't sad anymore. I wanted to be like him, as quickly as possible. I had no patience to wait.

Dad subscribed to classic psychoanalysis. He was the last of its followers, and despised modern, abbreviated, dynamic styles of therapy. "Advice givers"—that was his belittling nickname for therapists who utilized those methods. If you haven't reached all the way down to the deepest wound, uncovered it, and treated it, Dad said, you haven't done a thing. Sometimes it takes five hours, other times it takes five years, and sometimes you never get there at all, but one mustn't rush or look for shortcuts.

I didn't feel like seeing Dad just then. I'd leave him the fruit and go. I knew his sessions ended at a quarter of the hour, and it was now twenty till. I bit into one of the pretty peaches I'd bought him and some juice dripped down my chin. I left a note on the coffee table: *Dad, I stopped by. Hope you enjoy the fruit.* Then I closed the door quietly behind me.

*

Shauli called me almost every evening during the first days of basic training. They were allotted a few minutes of freedom before evening formation. I could hear in his voice that he wasn't broken, but he wasn't happy either. I asked what they were eating and if they were being pushed around a lot, what his new friends' names were, and if they'd received their rifles yet. As I listened to his brief answers, I asked myself why they were allowed to call home every night. It only served to weaken them, and in the meantime he was in no danger. These daily calls, like a kid phoning home from camp, made it harder for both of us. It would have been best if he used his free time to rest or buy himself a snack.

The first time I sent him off to kindergarten, a bad kid picked on him, bugging him and biting him. He would come home with tooth marks on his arm every day. I spoke to the teacher, but she just talked circles around me and did nothing about it. I had no choice but to teach Shauli to fight back. He was a small, soft child, not yet three, and I was already showing him how to throw a punch, pull hair, and bite back. I brainwashed him to give his bully hell next time. "Give him hell," he repeated in his childish voice, laughing.

The day the teacher came complaining that Shauli hit the bully, and that I had to do something about it, and when his upset mother called me later to scream at me (I politely told her where to go), I was relieved. I knew Shauli had learned how to survive.

"Good night, sweetheart, be strong," I'd say to him on the phone during the first weeks of basic training, until he stopped calling. That didn't concern me. He knew I loved him.

I was giving a talk to a new class of battalion commander training officers, one of the pleasurable tasks I kept after my discharge. Most of the training officers were in their late twenties, nearing thirty; young, ambitious, authoritative men. This time there was one female officer among them, I pointed out to myself. They watched me curiously as I stood there in skirt and heels. I'd spent a long time in front of my closet that morning, picking out the right outfit. For the next few months, I'd come talk to them once a week—my famous class on military psychology.

"When I was twenty-five years old," I told them, "having completed two psychology degrees as part of military academic studies, I was assigned a role as psychologist of a paratrooper brigade. A mental health officer. I was given a small office with a desk and two chairs and was expected to interview problematic soldiers and determine who was actually losing it and who was just trying to get an early discharge. I got bored very quickly. A few weeks in, I went to see the brigade commander and told him I wanted to go out to the field and spend some time with the soldiers.

"He looked at me like I'd just landed from outer space. 'No one before you has ever gone out into the field. What do you have to look for out there?'

"I explained that I wanted to see how the soldiers lived, to get to know their roles and the pressures they were under. How else was I supposed to understand their souls? He agreed to let me join a training session in the Golan Heights for three days. The name of the battalion commander who hosted me there might ring a bell. Lieutenant Colonel Rosolio, who is now the Chief of Staff. He was more or less the age you are now, and when I showed up he looked at me the way you're looking at me now, like, *What does this girl want from me?* I explained that I had no intention of getting in his way. I was just there to learn.

"The wheels in his brain turned quickly. 'Welcome,' he said. 'Come on, we're about to head out for a drill. Hurry up, we're about to start.'

"Before I could even put down my pack, he had me get in his jeep and we headed out into the field. As we drove, he explained what was going on, which force was performing the main maneuver, who was running diversion, and where the suppressive fire was. I ran with him and the signaler among the boulders. He took no mercy on me. I fell down twice, and when the drill was over a few hours later, I was covered in sweat, my makeup running. But we'd conquered our target. We won. Even though there was no real enemy, I felt the joy of triumph. Then we returned to camp, dined on field rations, and I stayed the night. Not to worry, I was set up with a cot in the women's tent, and even a separate shower with a little bit of hot water. They were perfect gentlemen. That evening, as I was getting ready for bed, Rosolio sent a soldier to get me, and I followed. Rosolio was sitting outside his tent with the other officers and a few old-timer NCOs. They had a small fire going and were making coffee, and Rosolio asked me to sit with them. Speaking softly, so as not to wake up the sleeping soldiers, they told funny stories of their military days, about odd characters they'd encountered, peculiar commanders, ridiculous missions.

Not great tales of bravery, just amusing anecdotes. The conversation went around in circles, everybody sharing, except for me. I was too embarrassed to talk. What could I possibly tell them? About my time at the university? The nights and days I spent poring over books? But they wouldn't let me get out of it. 'Your turn to share something,' they insisted, and I froze, until Rosolio came to my rescue. 'Do some kind of psychology trick for us,' he said. 'Can you interpret dreams?'

"My stomach turned as if I'd given a pop quiz. Above me was the sea of stars, and all around me was a group of strange men. 'Sure I know how to interpret dreams. I'm an expert on Freud,' I said.

"'Great. Who's got a dream for the mental health officer?' Rosolio asked.

"One of the young officers raised his hand and shared a dream he'd had a few nights earlier. In the dream, he was chasing down a wild boar through a field when suddenly he found himself deep in the woods, lost. He saw lights in the distance but couldn't reach them, and when he kept walking through the forest somebody pounced on him from behind and latched onto his back. A heavy man, apelike, his face rough and covered with hard stubble, a kind of prehistoric man. 'I walked through the woods with this guy on my back for half a night. I couldn't shake him off. We almost became one person.'

"'How did you feel about him?' I asked.

"'He weighed me down and frightened me, but I gradually got used to him. When I woke up the next morning I looked for him in bed. I was convinced he was still there. When I couldn't find him I felt kind of disappointed.'

"There was a moment of awed silence, and then everybody started laughing.

"'Calm down a second,' Rosolio hushed them. He wanted to hear my thoughts.

"I asked the dreamer a few questions about his life. Where he lived, what kind of relationship he had with wild boars. He told me that people hunted them on the kibbutz where he lived. Now I had enough background in order to interpret the dream according to good old Dr. Freud's guidelines, though my interpretation was very shallow. After all, I knew basically nothing about this officer. 'This is a dream about growing up,' I said. 'You left home and you can't go back. You rely on yourself now. You're becoming tougher and cruder in order to survive, to catch prey. It frightens you. You want to get rid of this new man, to be light and carefree like you used to be. But on the other hand, you're attached to him. You're in transition. Don't let this savage take over you, but don't banish him, either. Be his friend. He'll keep you safe. Keep the good things about him. You had a very good, useful dream. Well done.'

"Everyone got excited, including Rosolio. Some people even clapped. I'd earned my spot by the fire. Others shared their dreams next. I became the center of attention, a kind of battalion clairvoyant.

"We laughed and enjoyed ourselves until one of Rosolio's company commanders shared his dream. Everyone fell silent when he started talking. It was a dream he had almost every night: he was climbing a steep cliff, tied to a safety harness, so that even if he lost his grip, he wouldn't fall. But then he realized his harness was gone and he was dangling over an abyss, barely hanging on to grooves in the rock face, his toes trying and failing to find notches to cling to. His energy ran out and he knew he would soon fall from a great height, with nobody around him to help.

"Everyone kept silent as the company commander told us his dream. We could practically see him falling. There wasn't much to interpret here besides the obvious—a terrible anxiety. When the guy finished talking, Rosolio walked over to him, put his hand on his shoulder, and told him he would never be alone, that they'd always help each other. But the guy was killed in an accident before he even turned thirty. Rosolio called me especially to tell me about it and ask if I remembered the man's dream. Of course I remembered. I remembered everything about that night.

"The next day, Rosolio let me speak to the soldiers. We sat on the ground under a tarp. When psychoanalysis was invented in Vienna, this was not what they had in mind. I spoke to young soldiers, to sergeants, to the guys from the assisting company. I talked to all of them. It was riveting. In my mind, the battalion became a living creature, with many heads, arms, and eyes. Those three days were my gateway into the soul of the military. After that, I went out into the field many more times. I didn't wait for them to come see me on the verge of collapse. I didn't stay in my tiny office, behind my desk. Over time, they got used to me. The commanders liked my visits and appreciated being able to get my advice on how to improve motivation and handle disciplinary issues, boost cohesiveness within the force and communication between units. I had lots of theoretical knowledge on these topics, and it was fascinating to implement it in the field. The soldiers discussed everything with me—homesickness, the mental challenges of such a demanding service, their romantic relationships and unrequited loves. Fear was present in every conversation with them, even when they didn't name it. I knew I had to feel it myself. I couldn't leave it in the realm of theory.

"A few months later, Rosolio's battalion settled in Lebanon, and I requested permission to visit. The brigade commander refused. He said there was no point in putting me at risk, that it would be an unnecessary burden on the force that would need to take care of me. But I insisted, and spoke to Rosolio, who persuaded the brigade commander. I remember how I felt when we crossed the border. My stomach tingled as if I were embarking on a pleasant adventure. I was driven by truck to Rosolio's post, deep inside Lebanon, and I stayed for a week. The first night, we were bombed with mortar shells. I was frightened, but trusted the people around me to keep me safe. That's where I understood the meaning of fighters' camaraderie and felt its force. I'll put it another way: professionally speaking, that's where I lost my objectivity. I became one of them. That's a dangerous thing for a psychologist to say, but there it is. On my third morning, we heard a loud explosion nearby. A recon tour came across an explosive device while clearing the road. Rosolio headed there immediately. I got into his car without asking permission. I'll never forget what I saw when we got there: a soldier sitting on the road, one leg missing, helmet removed, his face very pale. The doctor who had come with us from the post ran over and tried to stop the bleeding. Soldiers kneeled on both sides of the road with their vests, helmets, and rifles. I felt something freezing in time, as if the image was staged. Everybody's thoughts were hanging in midair. The sky was bright and the air was clear, and I took it all in with frightening clarity. The chopper arrived, we heard it approaching. It evacuated the soldier back to Israel. When the soldiers returned to the post, Rosolio convened them and asked me to join too. They were young, nineteen or twenty. I didn't know exactly what to tell them, how to reassure them. I operated according to instinct. It was the first time I'd had to treat trauma in real time, and everything I did afterward began there. Rosolio started talking, and I slowly and quietly joined in like an orchestral accompaniment. Rosolio asked about the operational details, and I asked how they felt. I asked them to tell me about their friend who was injured. Some of the soldiers started to cry. Their company commander rebuked them, urging them to behave like men, but Rosolio told him to let them cry. As far as I know, this was the first time the IDF had run a questioning in the presence of a psychologist immediately following battle, rather than waiting a few weeks to conduct it back on the home front, when the trauma had already become embedded and was too difficult to treat. As soon as the discussion was over, Rosolio sent them to do recon on the same road. We had them operative again immediately. I was glad I'd been around to help.

"When Rosolio was promoted to brigade commander a few months later, he invited me to his office and asked me a very direct question: how could I help him make the soldiers better fighters? I asked what being better fighters meant. He explained: functioning better in battle, with minimal hesitation and fear. I asked: *Do you mean you want them to be able to kill more easily?* He answered simply, *Yes.*

"I asked Rosolio to let me spend a month doing research at the university library and then get back to him with answers. He agreed. Thus began my romance with the psychology of killing. A new world had opened up to me. A month later, I presented the essentials of what I'd learned to Rosolio, and—at his request—wrote a paper that many commanders found eye-opening. I ask that all of you read it before our next session. There are copies at the door to grab on your way out.

"After that, the military sent me for a two-month course at the Marine Military Academy in Texas. I studied with the top military psychologists in America who spend all of their time researching ways to optimize the lethality of their organization. They've got plenty of experience from their empire's many wars. When I got back, I gave a talk to the senior command staff, and every combat unit came knocking on my door, asking me to consult for them. This is who I am, this is what I'm going to teach you, and I hope you find it useful and interesting," I said, walking out of the lecture hall with my back straight. I was pleased. I felt I'd left the right impression.

What I didn't tell them, nor had any intention of telling them, was that when I was thirty-three years old, after having served as a mental health officer for the paratrooper brigade and the elite General Staff Reconnaissance Unit, I seduced Rosolio because I'd decided I wanted to have a child with him. He was almost forty years old, married with two daughters, and had never touched me until then, even though we'd been working together for years. There were a few moments when an emotional intimacy had developed between us, when I advised him and supported him in times of need. He was a master of self-discipline, never saying a word about it, but he couldn't contain the look in his eyes, and I could tell he wanted to.

At the time, Rosolio was in charge of a series of extremely secretive operations, during one of which our soldiers were almost caught in an enemy country, getting out by sheer luck and the skin of their teeth. Rosolio asked me to get involved and meet the fighters because the atmosphere was becoming panicked, and he was concerned that this panic could lead to failure. He could sense fear walking among them like a deadly virus. I came to their base right away, spoke to the commanders, and designed an action plan together with them. Then I met the teams for one-on-one and group sessions, and the change was apparent in a matter of days. They were ready to go back to business as usual. Rosolio was grateful. His career hinged on the success of this mission, and his nerves were shot by the time I'd arrived. He was good at hiding it behind his cool exterior, but I saw right through him.

Whenever I asked myself who I wanted to be the father of my child, all I could see was Rosolio. It's impossible, I told myself. I tried to erase him from my mind, but he kept popping up—in my dreams, when I was awake, in explicit visions. Finally, I decided to take a chance: one congress, one cosmic clash. Whatever happens, happens.

The time came on my final night working with his unit, after questioning the last team to return from the field. It was a victory celebration, though Rosolio attempted to keep things restrained. We parted with an elated sense of success, the Minister of Defense delivering a special thank-you note, someone pouring whiskey into plastic cups, and everyone sending me off with affection and appreciation, like I was one of their own.

Nighttime. Rosolio walked me to my car. We were both in high spirits, enveloped by the aroma of orchards and summer, walking close together. He put his hand on my shoulder for a moment, and my breath caught—don't back down now, this is the moment. No one was around, and yet he started and removed his hand. I took it in mine and decisively returned it to my shoulder. Then, to break the awkwardness, I said, "What a lovely night." He mumbled something back, shaken, clearly unused to this kind of thing. He was a loyal man, Rosolio. I was afraid he'd slip between my fingers.

"Why don't we go to your room," I said. I knew he'd been allotted a little chamber for the purposes of this operation, in a distant corner of the camp, within a eucalyptus thicket. We could slip in there without anyone noticing. We snuck over softly, made sure no one was around, and when he locked the door behind us we both burst out laughing, and I knew things would go my way. I didn't have to work too hard to seduce him. I got what I wanted from him between his single bed and the shower. A moment before he entered me, I told him I wasn't using any protection, and that I wanted a baby from him. A moment's hesitation passed over his face. Then he said, "All right, I understand," and continued to touch me. I think that was a very decent move on my part.

In the middle of the night, when we got up to leave, he caressed me gently and said some kind words that I still remember. His face was serene. I felt good with him too. As I drove back into town through empty roads, I felt I was carrying a treasure within me.

A few weeks later, when I was certain of it, I made an appointment with him. I told him I was pregnant. "I went back and forth about it a few times," I lied, "and I want to keep it."

He nodded, and without having to demand it, I made a commitment to him: I would never tell anybody he was the father, not even the child. I wouldn't ask for money. He wouldn't have to play any part in this child's life.

"Are you asking permission?" he asked.

"No," I said. "I want this very badly."

"All right," he said again. "I understand."

We stuck to our agreement. We didn't meet again while I was pregnant. I fought myself every day, literally digging my fingernails into my arm to stop myself from calling him, from seducing him again with my beautiful pregnancy, my round belly and full breasts, all this glory he'd created. My mother was the only person with me in the delivery room, and she didn't ask any questions. My parents helped me raise Shauli from the very beginning. My mother took care of him for many full days, and did so gladly. Shauli's birth brought a light into her life.

On Shauli's first day of first grade, I sent a picture of him with his new backpack and happy smile to Rosolio. I couldn't resist. It was a one-time indiscretion, hasty and careless. I hoped he'd delete the picture and ignore the message, but he responded right away: "Sweet child. Enjoy him, they grow up fast." For hours, my eyes caressed the words he'd written. Not writing him back was torture.

4

NOGA TEXTED that she was going to be in town this weekend and asked if I wanted to meet up. *How about we get a drink at your spot on Thursday night?*

Sure, I replied. There was a small bar just around the corner from my apartment that I had once mentioned during therapy, which her quick brain had retained. During my long university years, when I was still living with my parents, I went there to breathe a different kind of air. I'd have a couple of drinks and get chatted up by older men, whom I almost always turned down cordially. The owner took me under his wing. A few years ago, he had a stroke and his speech was affected, but he still came by every night and made music selections—mostly jazz. His daughter, who was about my age, poured drinks. They both always looked at me kindly.

I sat at the edge of the bar, my regular spot, and saw Noga walking in, wearing jeans, a T-shirt, and dainty sneakers, her eyes adjusting to the darkness. She searched for me awkwardly, and a few of the aging regulars looked up with surprise. Young people hardly ever came here. I stood up to greet her.

"It's dark here," she said, flashing me her brilliant smile.

I'd missed her. She cheered my heart. "This is like my second home," I said. "These people have raised me since I was nineteen."

The owner smiled at us silently from the other end of the bar.

"You've lost a lot of weight," I said when she took a seat next to me.

Noga laughed and said she'd actually gained some weight. She was eating too much bread and cake, there was always some kind of celebration going at the squadron.

This was our first meeting outside of my clinic. I thought I might have made a mistake, agreeing to meet at such a public place.

The bartender asked her amiably what she wanted to drink, and when Noga hesitated, the bartender offered to make her something she'd like.

"You can trust her," I said.

"What do you like? Sweet, bitter, or sour?" the bartender asked.

Noga smiled and said a little of everything, but mostly sweet.

We'd had our final session two months earlier, having made a mutual decision that she'd had enough therapy for the moment and that my door was open whenever she needed me. Then I started missing her, and texted her that I would love to get together.

"Me too," she responded.

And that's how we found ourselves in a dark corner of the bar, drinking cocktails. The alcohol softened me, and I even felt affection toward the aging losers all around, some of whom had tried and failed to pick me up thirty years earlier, and who now served as the backdrop to our evening. I was given an hour with this wondrous, state-of-the-art creature, and I was going to make the most of it.

"How are things at the squadron?" I asked.

Noga told me that her training period was over and she was now fully implemented in the shift schedule. "I launched this week," she carried on lightly, as if recounting a hike she'd taken, her speech lilting gracefully. "We hit a rocket factory. I fit the missile in through the window. Everyone was very happy for me. When we landed, they sprayed me with sparkling wine to celebrate my first time."

I hummed my understanding. That was my father's habit, which I'd picked up and couldn't quit. "How did that feel?" I asked, and realized from the look in her eyes that I'd made a mistake. She didn't want me to treat her, to hum, or to ask her how things felt. Billie Holiday wailed sweetly, and the owner glanced at me with wise warmth as his daughter poured me another gin and tonic. She knew what I liked.

Noga froze on the barstool, her eyes looking for an escape route, and I knew I had to change the subject before she fled. "How's your new apartment?" I asked, picking an innocent question.

"Great," Noga said, smiling again. Her neck was long and dainty, her skin clear and whole. "The kitchen sink is leaking, the place is swarming with mosquitos, the paint is peeling in the bathroom, and it costs as much as an eight-bedroom villa back in the village, but we're having a great time. Finally living in the city, away from my parents. Even though I barely make it over to the apartment, maybe once or twice a week, when I'm not on duty. That's what all the boys do, so it was silly for me to be the only one who stays on base all week."

"How's your roommate?" I asked.

"We're like two little girls left home alone," Noga laughed. "We hardly see each other. She's very busy too, always studying or working. Sometimes her boyfriend spends the night and I have to press a pillow over my head to block out the sound, but I don't care. I know she's been waiting for this a long time."

We had a few more drinks. The bartender treated us well. I rarely drank this much. I never let myself lose control. But I wanted to show Noga I wasn't her therapist anymore, I was her friend, and we could drink and laugh together about frivolous stuff, me and my golden girl.

It had been a year since the captivity training where we'd met. After that, Noga completed her course, got her wing pin, and was appointed to a fighter chopper squadron. From time to time I got in touch with my contacts in the air force and asked about her. I was told she was doing fine, progressing nicely. The incident that had taken place during captivity training had been forgotten everywhere except for in my clinic, where the two of us processed it from every possible angle. No one knew she was in therapy. We met every time she had leave, even on weekends and holidays, if need be, until I assured myself she was fine and that I could let go.

"Shauli enlisted," I told her under the purple lights of the bar. She asked how I felt, and I said I wasn't sleeping well, even though he wasn't in any danger yet. She liked the drink the bartender had made her, and her eyes glittered. I used to beam like that when I was her age, as brilliantly and quickly, but I lacked the physical and mental courage to stride ahead on my own. I was close to taking off, but I blocked myself, depending instead on strong men to pull me along. My engine wasn't prepared for takeoff. That's why it was so important to me not to let Noga crash.

By the time we left the bar it was almost midnight. I lit my once-a-day cigarette. We walked down the street together, laughing. We were friends now. I recalled the desperate look in her eyes back in captivity training, when I had pulled her out of the interrogation room, filthy. Noga said she had to be back on base early the next morning and offered to walk me home, because I was tipsy and swaying a little.

"That's all right, dear, it's just a couple minutes away, I'll be fine," I said. "Sleep well, kill the bad guys, and I'll see you again soon." I spread my arms for a tight hug. I wanted to give her strength. She boarded one of those electric scooters and sailed down the street, standing tall like a goddess. Did she want to sleep over? I suddenly blushed after she was gone. The thought agitated me.

One of the high points of my military service had been reimagining captivity training for elite units. Until then, the soldiers were taught to keep their mouths shut, offering no answers beyond their names and ranks, even if they were tortured to death. But over time and wars, the military realized this was not a realistic expectation, because most prisoners weren't like Uri Ilan, who committed suicide in a Syrian jail so as not to reveal state secrets. Even under the worst torture, they still wanted to live, and couldn't be expected not to talk at all. But the captivity training still fit the outdated ideal, and occasionally a young soldier broke under pressure. After a few of these sad incidents, the General Staff Commando Unit chief asked me to design a new training series. "It should still be tough," he instructed me, "so don't make it a spa day either."

I created a much more intelligent captivity training series for them, transforming it into a controllable nightmare with intervention options to prevent emotional collapse. I allowed the prisoners to talk without disclosing the most confidential information. The results were very good. Later, when we discussed the soldiers' experiences with them, it turned out that the desirable behavior had been internalized.

The air force contacted me a few years later, after I'd already been discharged, following the meltdown of a female pilot trainee. There was a ruckus, an inquiry committee had been put together, and a damages suit had been filed. Then my name came up. Had they asked me sooner, the entire ordeal might have been prevented. They asked me for specific advice on adapting the training for women. They asked me to study the specific pressures at work, their breaking points, and which adjustments should be made during captivity training. I didn't love that idea. I don't like to focus specifically on women. My specialty is soldier and military psychology, and I didn't want to limit myself. I told them I was retired, but when the Air Force Commander called me himself to ask for my help personally, I relented.

First I observed the female participants to understand who I was dealing with. I sat in the back of a classroom during a complicated Basics of Aviation class. Noga stood out to me right away, before I even knew a single detail about her, with her divine concentration, her wise expression, and the short and intelligent questions she asked the instructor. I knew that she would make it further than any of the other women in the room. Later, I read in her file that she came from a good family and a wealthy village, got terrific grades in high school, played basketball on the school team, was a leader in the Scouts, and passed every military classification exam with flying colors.

Then I interviewed each girl privately, waiting for Noga's turn to come. This is how a person ought to look and sound, I thought after speaking with her for a few minutes. She contained the perfect blend of intelligence and quiet charisma, occasionally offering a wise, innocent smile without a hint of malice. Her voice was young and slightly lilting in a captivating way. But in the middle of the interview I felt as if I were being slathered with maple syrup. I was too charmed by her. I decided to switch gears and challenge her. "You're very *nice*," I said, intentionally choosing that aggravating word. "Do you think you can be a fighter?"

That erased the smile from her young, red lips. "I hope so," she said. "I'm doing my best to learn the profession."

I removed my reading glasses and pressed her, without empathy. "Being an Air Force pilot is not a profession. It isn't like being a bus driver."

She considered this, then said, "All right, I accept that."

"Of course you accept it, Noga. I wasn't asking for your acceptance. Let me be clearer. Do you think you'll be capable of killing?" I asked sharply and angrily.

For the first time, she looked at me with a touch of distaste. *What's this old lady attacking me for?*

You're not here to make friends with this girl, I reminded myself.

"Yes, I'm capable of killing," Noga said.

"How can you be sure?" I insisted. "Have you ever killed anything bigger than a fly?"

"I actually don't kill flies," she smiled. Her hair was tied back and her eyes were filled with laughter. "I shoo them away. I only crush bloodsucking mosquitos."

"Then how do you know, Noga?"

"Do you ask boys this question too?" she countered. "Because I don't see any difference between me and the boys. I think I'll perform my missions just like they do."

I put my glasses back on, fixed my eyes on my papers, and told her to send in the next interviewee on her way out. She irked me for reasons that had nothing to do with her and everything to do with me. I wanted to crush her a little because she was so perfect, but I couldn't. For the moment, she had the upper hand. I let her go. She walked out of the room and sent the next girl in, and I immediately regretted being so mean. I had to stop myself from following her out and apologizing.

We met again a few weeks later, during captivity training. Noga was brought into the interrogation room in the late afternoon, and I watched her through the two-way mirror. It was a Sunday, and she had been abducted on her way to base early that morning, blindfolded, handcuffed, and shoved into a car that drove her in silence to a military detention center, an entire wing of which had been repurposed for this training. Her blindfold was removed only when she was pushed into a small cell that was typically used for solitary confinement. The guard threw a prisoner's uniform at her and ordered her in Arabic to change. He stayed in the cell with her as she removed her military uniform and put on the smelly prison garb. I allowed that, but forbade anyone from touching the female soldiers, even though we knew that when the time came they would be touched. That was a line I wouldn't allow anyone to cross. Even stripping down to their bras and underwear in the presence of a strange man was traumatic enough for these girls. We let her languish in the cell for ten hours before she was led into the interrogation room. It was almost evening, but she didn't know what time it was because all of her personal belongings had been taken from her, including her watch and her phone. Until that moment, no indication had been given to her that this was just a drill. Though the trainees knew the prison training series would inevitably come, at this point they were beginning to feel a hint of doubt. *Maybe this was the real thing?*

She walked into the interrogation room, head held high, face flinty. My impression was that she was doing all right—tense but in control. I asked myself if I would have been able to tolerate it, then pushed the thought away. I couldn't get distracted now. I was never the point.

She was seated on a low wooden chair across from the interrogators. There were two of them, borrowed from the Intelligence Branch, playing the part of enemy interrogators, speaking with a thick Arab accent. I could see her searching their faces for clues, signs that everything was all right, just a game. But they were awfully serious, diving into their roles. I hoped they wouldn't get too carried away, because she looked like an elegant bird caught in a trap.

A veteran reserve duty pilot was sitting beside me, biting his nails. "It's terrible, seeing a girl in this situation," he said before they'd even started.

The interrogators asked for her full name. She gave it to them. "Where do you serve?" they asked.

She said, "The Air Force."

"Where in the Air Force?" they asked. She gave the squadron number she was instructed to give. "What's your role?" asked the shorter of the two, clean-shaven with a prominent square jaw.

She said nothing, looking confused for the first time. Should she tell them she was a pilot?

"We've got intel," the taller, bearded interrogator said, raising his voice. "And we know you're a pilot."

"A pilot," she confirmed, no doubt recalling the detailed briefing they had been given a few weeks earlier.

"What kind of jets do you fly?" they asked.

"Choppers," she said.

"What's your mission?" they asked.

Noga said her mission was to protect the country. Things were going smoothly so far.

"What does that mean?" the bearded one asked.

"Fighting our enemies. Terrorists."

He got up and walked over to her, standing very close. She turned her face away, as if he smelled badly. That was a mistake. He ran his hand down her cheek. That was allowed. Then he said, "You won't be calling us terrorists again. You'll treat us with respect, you understand?"

"Yes," she said. I saw her swallowing an amused smile, as if she would be pulled out of there any minute now, game over.

"Now, tell us who you want to kill," the bearded one demanded. The shaved one was still standing close to her.

"I don't know," she said. "We're only given targets, I don't know their names." She was getting too close to dangerous territory, and the veteran pilot next to me put his head in his hands.

From behind the desk, the bearded interrogator asked, "Don't you care who you kill?"

The short one ran his hands through her shiny pony-tail, then gave it a little tug.

"Leave it," she protested. "Don't touch me."

"I'll touch you as much as I want," he said, continuing to pet her hair.

She pushed his hand away and he slapped her.

My breath caught. I allowed it. She could take it.

"Is that okay?" the pilot next to me said, startled.

"If she were one of the boys," I said, "would you still ask me the same question?"

We were someplace else now. A line had been crossed. The pride was wiped off her face. She folded into herself. The room was made intentionally cold and her clothing was thin. "I don't know who I kill, I'm sorry," she said weakly.

They asked her about the military's method of hitting targets. This was sensitive, perilous stuff, like quicksand. There were details that she could reveal, information anyone could find online. But the special techniques developed by the Air Force, combining intelligence with advanced weaponry, were confidential. The pilot next to me was on the edge of his seat. Noga stuttered. I could tell her brain was working overtime, her body emitting a cascade of fight-or-flight hormones, but she was trapped in a locked room with no chance of flight and no realistic way to fight these two stronger men with her bare hands. The shaved one rested his hand on the tender back of her neck and squeezed. "Answer," he said in Arabic. "Answer the question, bitch."

She bit her lips and started to describe how she aimed at a target without disclosing any secrets, just as she'd been trained.

"No, that's not what I asked you!" the bearded one shouted. "I asked how you know where a target is. How do they mark it? Who gives you the information?"

Noga's eyes bounced around, seeking help. No help is coming, dear, I thought. You wanted to be a pilot. There are no shortcuts for women. "I can't answer that," she said, flinching like a scared snail.

The clean-shaven one spat into her face. That was the guidance I'd given them. Spit doesn't kill anyone. She wiped it off with her sleeve. Now she lowered her head and we couldn't see her face.

"Don't you want to intervene now?" the reserve-duty pilot asked, frightened.

"Not yet," I said.

"Answer us, who gives you the targets?" the bearded one asked, hardly moving from his seat. The little guy was in charge of choreography.

"I don't know," she said.

The short guy walked over to the tall guy and said something quietly, in Arabic. I was also feeling uncomfortable at this point.

"Tie her up," the bearded one told him in Hebrew. They were playing the game well and I could tell they were enjoying it.

"Put your hands behind your back," the short one said, binding them together with cable ties behind the back of the chair.

"It hurts," she said.

He told her this was only the beginning, and if she didn't start talking things would get much worse. Now her shoulders were arched backward. It was a very uncomfortable position. I tried it once when I was planning this training. I thought about the dance and athletics classes her parents must have sent her to as a little girl, the dainty ballet outfit, the tender Chopin music.

"I need to go to the bathroom," she said.

"No bathroom until you tell us how you kill people," the tall one said quietly.

She said nothing.

"You got a boyfriend?" the little guy asked, running his hand down her cheek again.

She couldn't resist this time. "No," she said.

"A virgin," he told his friend, chuckling.

"Don't the pilots over there get laid?" the bearded one asked.

"Make it stop," the pilot sitting next to me said. "Go in there, right now. I can't watch this."

I shook my head and said, "It would be much worse in reality, it's our duty to prepare her."

They demanded that she answer their question again.

"I want to get out of here. Get my commanders. I don't want to stay here," Noga said.

"You aren't going anywhere, baby, we've got you for as long as we want and we haven't even started yet. We're your commanders now."

The little guy with the smooth cheeks was the first to notice the urine stain spreading across her pants and looked at the wall we were sitting behind. He was startled too and sought guidance. The bigger guy didn't notice and kept pressing her. A few seconds later there was a small puddle dripping underneath her. "Let me go," she said, barely audible. "I give up, I can't take it anymore."

The pilot gave me a reproachful look, but I didn't need it. I realized this had gone too far and that if I didn't intervene right away we were going to lose her. I got up quickly and walked into the interrogation room through the side door. The fake interrogators moved aside, embarrassed. "Untie her," I ordered them. She didn't move, sitting over the puddle of urine. "Noga," I said. "Noga, look at me."

She looked up, her eyes filled with hard, angry tears.

You broke her, I told myself, satisfied. I was ashamed of that thought. "Come with me," I said softly.

"I don't want to," she sobbed, her face twisted with anger and insult. "Look at what you did to me."

I helped her up, holding her hand as if she were my own daughter. I signaled to the others to look away and led her to the quiet room down the hall we'd prepared for this kind of situation. I pointed her to the adjacent bathroom and gave her a clean uniform.

"I want to go home," she said. "This is the worst moment of my life. I don't want to stay here anymore."

"Go take a shower and we can talk afterward," I told her. It took some effort, but I didn't yield to the temptation to torture myself with self-blame. I was there to handle the situation. That's exactly what I was invited to do. Lessons could be learned later.

"No, there's nothing to talk about. I want to sign the waiver and get out of here," she insisted.

Now I was on alert. I had to rescue her. "The nightmare is over, Noga," I said, "and you withstood it with courage."

"No, it isn't over," she said, shaking her head fiercely. Her face was red with tears and insult. She was in no rush to get in the shower and her pants continued dripping on the floor, a symbol of her humiliation. "Why did you do this to me?" she asked. "Did you come here to ruin my life?"

I could have explained it. I had all the appropriate excuses. But I decided to go off script. I put my arms around her and held her close. She got me damp, but I didn't care. She stood there, limp, ruined, and I kept holding her until her head fell against my shoulder and her hands found my back and gripped me tightly. "I'm sorry," I whispered. "I'm sorry about all this shit." She held me tighter, saying nothing. She was my daughter, my sister, myself. We stood like that for several minutes, the most intimate moment I've experienced in my entire life. "Go take a shower," I whispered, and she did. I stood behind the door, listening, occasionally asking if she was all right, making sure she wasn't hurting herself. I told myself that we ought to install security cameras in the bathroom. But she stepped outside clean and neat, wearing a fresh uniform, her hair tied back, only her eyes still sad and red. I told her to go eat something and get some rest.

"Are they going to kick me out because of this?" she asked as we said goodbye.

"I'll take care of you," I promised.

The next day, we concluded the training in a long meeting at the course commander's office. We listed the trainees one by one. Most of them had come out unscathed. Our mission had been accomplished. If they were ever captured by enemy forces, they'd have a better chance of survival, and the military could rest assured that its secrets were safe. But when we reached Noga's name we lingered.

"I don't think she's a good fit," the veteran pilot who'd been sitting next to me during the training said plainly. He thought Noga was too fragile and wouldn't be able to handle the pressures of military action, and that if she ever was taken captive, then heaven help us. "She just isn't built for it. She totally fell apart in that room," he said.

A large screen played her hardest moments, right until the point when I came in to get her. There were only a few weeks left of the course, and until that point Noga had been a star student, and yet the opinion in the room was leaning against her. They wanted her out. I held off from speaking until the end, then utilized all of my professional authority to convince them they had nothing to be afraid of. She was a strong girl, and her behavior during this training had no bearing on how she would function as a pilot. "She'll be perfect," I promised. "This is a unique situation, and we must have pressured her too much. It's my fault, I should have intervened sooner. We can do better next time, but for now, she shouldn't be the one to pay the price." I knew I was gambling on her life as well as my professional reputation, but I'd made a promise to her.

After a long discussion, they softened and accepted my opinion as the training's top psychological authority. "We're holding you accountable, this girl is your responsibility," the course commander said, giving me a hard look.

I hoped I wasn't making a fateful mistake. When I left the meeting, before heading back into town, I found her in the women's barracks. She was waiting there for our verdict. I told her she was staying. "I convinced them," I said.

Her smile was grateful, but sad too.

"But there are strings attached," I said, making up the strings without asking anyone's permission. "We have to stay in touch. You have to come see me. I can help."

"Of course," Noga said, nodding vigorously. "I want to stay in touch. I want to see you."

"Do you want to stay? To be a pilot?" I asked.

"Yes, very much." She stood before me, lithe and stubborn, arms pinned against her body as if at attention.

You break them down and then try to fix them, I told myself on the car ride home. Like some psychopathic toy collector. Thank God your father didn't see what you did here. But that's the job, I corrected myself sternly. That's what these kids want, and I'm helping them achieve their goals. They're addicted to hardship and misery. She was free to run. She could have given up at any moment. Nobody was stopping her, certainly not me.

5

"HUMAN BEINGS are tenderhearted." That's how I started my second talk with the battalion commander trainees. "Most of them flinch at the thought of killing, except for the few who were born to do it, for whom killing comes naturally. The military's purpose is to teach the soft majority how to kill."

I was wearing a blue dress that came down to just above my knees. I knew I was still able to capture their attention by merely standing before them, even though they were a generation younger than me. I wore a little makeup. I wanted to look glowing. The presentation beamed against the screen. I explained the principles of the psychology of killing. I told them that in-depth, broad-scope studies conducted by the American military during World War II had made the surprising discovery that only twenty percent of army soldiers shot the enemy with an intent to kill. The others either didn't shoot at all, or shot into the air. The officers sitting in the audience looked at the slide without much surprise. Unlike the public at large, which didn't understand the meaning of war, this crowd got it. I told them the American army had drawn conclusions from these studies, utilized the help of psychologists, and transformed their training methods. A couple of decades later, during the Vietnam War, more than eighty percent of army soldiers were shooting with an intent to kill.

"But that didn't help them win Vietnam," a bespectacled artillery officer sitting in the back said. He seemed pleased with his insight. "On the other hand they won World War II, big-time."

"They killed over two million people in Vietnam. Their killing capabilities had improved tremendously," I said. "There were other reasons they didn't win. That's a fact, you can't argue with that."

"But what good were those piles of corpses if they ended up losing the war?" the artillery officer asked. There was always one guy who tried to drag the discussion in a different direction.

"They lost because they didn't have faith in their cause," one of the course commanders, sitting right in front of me, said. "That's the main conclusion from Vietnam."

"And what about us?" the artillerist asked.

"That's a good question," I said. "We haven't conducted such thorough research, and it's been a while since we've fought a real war, a big one, to test these things out. What's your intuition? What are our numbers like?"

I'd started a discussion. They whispered among themselves. I called on an officer who had a black Armored Corps beret under his epaulet.

"We always try to hit the target," he said. "I don't know any stories about people shooting into the air on purpose, or not shooting at all. It sounds very strange to me. Unbelievable."

"You're right," I said. "Shooting from a tank is completely different from shooting from close range." I moved to the next slide, which showed that readiness to kill increased the farther the target. "Inhibitions diminish from a distance," I explained. "When you can't see the enemy's face, when you can't smell them, when you don't have to consider their humanity, things are much easier. Killing from jets, tanks, cannons—there are almost no psychological issues with those. Killing with missiles is child's play, almost like a video game."

The Armored Corps officer wasn't totally satisfied with my explanation, which must have hurt his sense of his masculinity. He made a face but kept quiet. The others nodded in agreement. They knew what I was talking about. I asked myself which of these officers had killed people and which of them hesitated. I wanted to know who was capable of it; how many natural born killers I was dealing with. I was still searching for some primitive pattern in their features, though I knew I'd never find one. Even a heartless murderer can have the face of an angel.

"Every act of killing has an emotional toll," I continued. Here and there I caught the eyes of a young man staring at my legs or the line of my tight dress, and it gave me a boost. Nobody fell asleep or yawned at my lectures. I pulled up a picture of young Robert De Niro, bare-chested, pulling a gun on the mirror. "I'm sure you've seen the film *Taxi Driver*," I said. To my surprise, only a few of them nodded. "If you haven't, I recommend it. The protagonist is a Vietnam vet. Hundreds of thousands of American soldiers who served in Vietnam came back with post-traumatic stress disorder. Night terrors, painful memories, problems concentrating, chronic neuroticism, guilt, and depression. Many also came back with emotional damage from Iraq. The process of killing, as well as being the target of killing, leaves a deep scar on the mind, except in a rare few who were born to be fighters."

"Why do you keep going back to Vietnam? What about us?" the bespectacled artillerist asked again, making some of the others laugh. He was a joker. Far at the edge of the row sat the only female cadet in the course, watching me coldly, as if she was on to me.

"Things with us are more or less the same," I said. "Except our wars are shorter and smaller in scope. Thousands of our soldiers suffered shell shock after the Yom Kippur War, most of whom are still being treated," I answered directly. "Same goes for every war that followed, in Lebanon, Gaza, and the West Bank. Lots of mental illness. I meet them in my clinic every day. I imagine some of you have already participated in battle, so you know life isn't the same afterward."

Many nodded again, a gloomy chorus of men.

"Studies conducted within the IDF found that people who killed from close range, who looked into the enemy's eyes as they shot them in the head or burst their guts open, are especially prone to suffer traumatic memories. It stays with them until the end of their lives."

"So what would you have us do? Not kill? Be killed instead?" an officer with a Givati Brigade beret sitting in the back cried out, his face angry.

I was used to this question. It came up every time.

He carried on. "We're combat soldiers. We didn't come here to sit around in an office. This is our job, and I'd rather survive and live with trauma than die." A rustle rose among them.

"I completely agree," I said. I spoke assertively and confidently. This was the moment to project authority. "I'm not sure you quite understand why I'm here. I didn't come here to weaken you or scold you. I'm here to help you and your soldiers win the war, kill the enemy, and stay alive. I've been studying the minds of warriors for over twenty years. I know what needs to be done to make soldiers more lethal, more disciplined, and more immune to trauma. But for us to succeed, you have to understand what goes through a soldier's mind, your mind, when you have to kill another human being, or when they try to kill you. It's always a meaningful event, and it always leaves a mark."

"I've killed some terrorists," a soldier in the back interjected. He had a shorn head and pleasantly masculine features. I could tell he was a member of an elite unit. "From up close, not from a jet or a submarine. I shot them. I saw the guts and blood and all that. It wasn't pleasant, but I have to tell you, it didn't cause any trauma. I sleep well at night, no nightmares, and I'd do it again, no problem. It's not like I'm a serial killer, you can ask my friends and my wife. I'm a pretty normal guy, but I have no problem doing that. I shot the enemy. That's my job. They deserved it." All heads turned toward him as he spoke, then returned to me.

"You've got every chance to go far," I said, and everyone laughed. "No, I'm serious." I hushed them. "There's a small percentage of people like you, who don't agonize about killing, who don't feel remorse, who aren't tortured by memories. You're a positive sort of psychopath." Laughter again. "No, no," I continued. "I'm not joking, I'm sure you're a fantastic guy and that in normal life you would never hurt a fly. And I know the people you killed were villains who deserved it. You're a good soldier, and thank you for speaking so openly. The science of psychology has no complaints against you whatsoever. But be aware that even if your suppression mechanism is working well at the moment, that doesn't mean it will forever. Surprises happen. In a few years, you might find out that things aren't so simple anymore, and you aren't such a perfect psychopath after all."

He lowered his head and smiled to himself, and I thought about Mandy.

A few hands were raised in the audience, other people who had killed and wanted to talk about it. I let them speak. I was fascinated by their stories. Nobody admitted to suffering from nightmares or scruples, but I could detect the traces of trauma between the lines. The shadows of the people they'd killed were in the air, I could see them hovering over their shorn heads.

"We'll continue this next week," I told them when our time had run out, leaving them wanting more. When I stepped off the stage, some of them came over to surround me, asking questions, seeking my closeness. I knew that a few would call me later and ask for a remedy for their emotional anguish.

6

SHAULI CAME HOME that weekend. I was astonished when he appeared in the doorway with his uniform and rifle. I hadn't seen him in two weeks, and tried to complete the missing pieces with a single look. I treated him like a prince, doing my best to be the perfect mother. I cooked stews (I barely cook for myself—when he isn't around I mostly eat fruit and vegetables, yogurt, or some eggs at most), filled the fridge with his favorite foods, bought a challah for Shabbat, changed his sheets, and cleaned his room. He'd lost a lot of weight in the two weeks he'd been away. His hair was short, which suited him, and his face, neck, and arms were so tan they were almost black.

We sat at the dining table, I served him more and more food, and he told me about his friends, his commanders, the shooting ranges and morning formation. He's fine, I told myself, no cause for concern.

The channels of communication are open and his eyes aren't crying for help. I memorized the names of his new friends, just like I used to when he was in kindergarten. I nodded and smiled, riveted, listening as carefully as I could. Nothing existed beyond his face and his voice. Then he called up his friends, changed into a bathing suit, and grabbed his surfboard from his room. I asked if he wasn't exhausted. He said he was, but he didn't want to sleep the day away. After he left, I unpacked his things and carried the laundry bag over to the machine. Standing in front of the spinning clothes, I thought, The boy is back, everything is fine, he's healthy. For a moment, the cloud of worry hovering over my head scattered.

In the afternoon we walked over to my father's. He had ordered food from the last surviving Jewish restaurant in town—chicken soup, roast beef, and half a roast duck. He watched Shauli pick up a spoonful of chicken with noodles, and asked, "How are your feet? I had so much trouble with blisters and chafing when I was in the army. I remember it made my life a living hell. The boots were so heavy."

"I'm fine," Shauli said, smiling at his grandfather. "They gave us lighter shoes. And I'm having no problem with the physical activity. I'm even helping others."

"And how are your commanders? Are they very tough?" Dad asked.

"Yes," Shauli said, his mouth full. "They're tough. You can't joke around with them. One time, during formation, I once answered 'okay' instead of 'yes, sir' to a sergeant and had to run around the entire base with a full pack on my back."

"Don't worry," I said. "By the end of basic training, they'll be your friends. It's just a game they're playing with you."

"A sadistic game," Dad commented, "and likely completely unnecessary. If it were up to me they would have stopped that kind of thing a long time ago." But no one asks you, Dad, I thought. You've never tried to change anything, and the military can't just give up this power dynamic, it's part of the deal.

"Are they letting you sleep at night?" Dad asked, sticking a fork into a browned duck leg and placing it on Shauli's plate. He poured himself some red wine, even though he wasn't allowed to have it, and I didn't say anything because his face was very pale and his days seemed numbered anyway.

"In principle we get six hours of sleep," Shauli said, "but in practice it comes down to less, because we have to shower and all that. We don't always get hot water.

And sometimes we have guard duty at night. We're tired all the time."

Dad gnawed on the other piece of duck, crushing the bone between his teeth. He didn't like the military and had bad memories from his own service. Once, when I was a kid, he told me his commanders had picked on him because they thought he was a smart-ass.

"Your mother has good connections in the army," Dad said, and I could tell by his voice he was trying to provoke me. "Maybe she can talk to someone and get them to let you sleep a little more."

"You know I'm not going to do that, and Shauli doesn't want that either, it would only embarrass him," I retorted, getting pulled into his ruse.

"You've advised generals and colonels about how to get the most out of simple soldiers," Dad hissed. "You've translated capitalism into military terms, just like psychologists who work for factory owners do. But soldiers don't have a workers' union, so the army can do whatever it wants with them, even send them off to die."

"Is this really necessary?" I murmured, astounded by this burst of aggression.

Dad raised his eyes, which saw all—he knew how to paralyze me with those eyes—and said, "You're right, Abigail. It's a shame to spoil this delicious food."

Shauli buried his face in the plate and said nothing. He loved his grandfather very much, and the friction between us wasn't his problem, yet I was secretly angry with him for not coming to my defense, for always remaining neutral.

When I told my father, at age seventeen, that I'd applied to psychology studies as part of my military service, he tried to talk me out of it. "It's a dangerous combination of psychology and army," he said. To this day, I can hear his measured tone. "It's the greatest contradiction imaginable. The military is a totalitarian cohesion that erases the individual, and in our profession the individual is all that exists, and your loyalty toward them must be absolute. What are you hoping to achieve?"

I had no idea what I was hoping to achieve. I knew I wanted to be like Dad, better than Dad, and was looking for the quickest way there. I had no patience to wait until my service was over. I was still no match for Dad when it came to abstract ideas. He'd read all the English and French books that filled the shelves of his clinic, and I wasn't even out of high school yet. But I stood strong before him, not backing down, knowing intuitively that this was the right call. His resistance only reinforced me.

*

When I got my first military appointment as psychologist to the paratrooper brigade, I came over, proud and excited, to share my experiences. I felt like I was discovering the world. I wanted to tell him all about it and hear his thoughts. But he listened to me like he would a patient, not a daughter or even a colleague, offering no response.

"Dad," I finally said, "don't you have anything to say?"

He answered my question with his own, his voice low and severe. "Who do you work for?"

"I treat soldiers," I said.

"To what end?"

"Exactly the same way you treat civilians, Dad. Don't act like you don't know that."

"But what is the end goal?" he insisted. "Why does the paratrooper brigade need a psychologist?"

His mental prowess frightened me. He saw a few steps ahead, and I still couldn't. "To beat the enemy," I said directly. I wasn't about to play his game, so I intentionally offered the most mean-spirited response, knowing it would infuriate him.

"There, you've said it yourself," he said, turning his back on me. "What's that got to do with psychology?"

After that, I avoided talking shop with Dad, and since working for the military was such a major part of my life, it was like a chasm had opened up between us. I continued to love and admire him, to envy him, to compete against him, carrying him with me in everything I did. But ultimately I went out into the world to forge my own path, and he stayed back in his little clinic at home, at the end of the hall, right past the kitchen, where he grew old along with his bourgeois patients. I knew he'd wanted more out of his life.

Now Dad got up from the table. I helped him clear the empty plates, and he walked slowly back from the kitchen, carrying a bowl of sweet fruit compote from the restaurant. We ate it voraciously and loudly. I missed Mom. She always knew how to break the tension between me and Dad with mundane chitchat. Without her, I was totally raw with him.

"Why don't you spend the night here, Shauli?" Dad asked.

Shauli apologized and said he had plans to go out with friends. His dark arms wrapped around his grandfather's fragile body. He hugged him and gave him a goodbye kiss on the cheek.

"I apologize for the fight," I told Shauli outside. "We shouldn't have spoiled your Friday night."

"No big deal, I'm used to it," he said. "I don't mind. I'm not going to be a psychologist, that's for sure."

I laughed, gave him some spending money, and he went off to meet his friends.

When I woke up the next morning Shauli was still in bed. I let him sleep till noon, then woke him up with a large plate of pancakes topped with butter. I sat across from him, drinking tea, and asked where he'd gone the previous night. He said he'd gone over with some other friends to a classmate's place.

"Were there any girls there?" I asked.

He asked me to lay off. Then he got dressed, grabbed his guitar, and said he was going to jam with his high school band. They had a show coming up in a few weeks and needed to rehearse.

While he was gone I ironed his uniform carefully. I loved the rough texture of the fatigues and tried to remove rifle grease stains. Then I sat around, waiting for him. You can't go on like this, I told myself. This loneliness, alone for entire weekends. My thoughts wandered to Noga. I wondered what she was doing now, if she was on base, at her parents' house, or in her apartment, not calling me. If I didn't have Shauli to take care of, I might have gone to Mandy's.

When Shauli came home in the evening, he was overcome with exhaustion and the end-of-leave blues. I asked if he'd enjoyed jamming with his friends and what they'd told him about their military experiences. He gave terse, minimal answers. I was sorry I couldn't go back to basic training instead of him. I would have done fine and saved him the heartache.

"Go to sleep, kid," I told him. "You have to wake up early tomorrow morning. It was great to be with you this weekend."

When I was little, my father had a famous patient, who always climbed the stairs in the dark so no one would recognize him. He was a minister in the government, one of the big ones. I don't know what his issues were. Dad was very strict about confidentiality. But he was moved by the man's stature. I remember he would announce when the important patient was about to arrive, so we knew not to step out of the living room or make a sound while he was there. We were used to that anyway. We never showed ourselves anywhere near the clinic or said a word when he was with a patient anyway.

"I've never seen you this excited about a patient," Mom told him.

That irritated him. All patients were meant to be equal to him, and now his human weakness had been exposed. But this patient, he'd boasted to Mom, entrusted him with big state secrets and other sensitive matters that obviously he couldn't divulge to us. For years, Dad had listened to the stories of his regular patients, which had become boring by this point, and now this important man had come to open a window into a world of greatness. Not only that, but he sought Dad's guidance, offering him a measure of control over his life and perhaps the life of the country as well.

One evening, when Dad and I were home alone, he warned me not to open the sliding door and not to dare turn up the volume on the radio, the television, or a record player. Then he waited by the door, listening for the doorbell. I saw the important man's silhouette enter and remove its hat. In his formal voice, Dad said, "Please come in." Then I heard footsteps and the clinic door closing behind them. I was eleven years old, I think. I quietly pushed the sliding door open and padded over to the clinic, leaning my ear against the door. I couldn't hear words, but for the first time I'd witnessed the music of a therapeutic conversation, the rolling, human, broken narrative of a patient, my father's succinct questions, and the secretive silence. I envied them and was upset to have been left out of it. Then I heard a screech, a piece of furniture shifting, and my father's voice grew louder and closer to the door. I scampered away on tiptoes, like

I'd learned to do in ballet class, to the safe haven beyond the sliding door.

Eventually, Dad told Mom that the important man had ended their sessions. His disappointment was evident.

"Did you cure him?" I asked, looking at my father with the naive pride of a child.

Dad rubbed my hair and answered with a sad smile, "Yes, he's all better now."

In the attic crawl space—behind a few suitcases, Shauli's old artwork that I never dared throw out, and some junk, I kept a sealed box filled with interviews conducted years ago with soldiers who'd returned from battle. Piles of tapes and transcripts of them describing the moments in which they'd faced enemies and killed them with a gun, a rifle, a hand grenade, or their bare hands. All types of close-range killings were documented there. I'd spoken to everyone, from simple soldiers to generals. Dozens of hours of deathly descriptions lying around like rotting meat. At the time, I'd published two articles on the topic in professional military journals. I named one "Principles in the Psychological Theory of Killing in Battle" and the other "Psychological Aspects in the Sniper's Work." I taught them in my courses, and a few of the more intelligent commanders read them. But my grand plan, which I had yet to fulfill, was to write a book, an important research tome that would be read by the public at large and would break me out of my shell, presenting me to the world. I'd neglected this project throughout the years. My day job always demanded too much. But now I had more free time, no more excuses, and still all of those materials were lying around up there like fossils.

I climbed the ladder to the highest rung and got on my tiptoes. The crawl space was dark and dirty, and I had to move all sorts of other objects in order to reach the box. I brought it down and was startled to find it damp. Some of the papers were already molding, but the tapes were carefully stored inside layers of plastic and most of the documents were still legible. Amos—I read from a random piece of paper, wiping away the sludge—an infantry fighter who'd participated in the First Lebanon War, was describing his encounter with a Syrian soldier who'd been staking him out. Luckily for Amos, the Syrian's rifle was jammed. He was about ten feet away and Amos cocked his weapon and was about to shoot when the Syrian yelled something and raised his arms in the air. He knew that the Syrian had planned to kill him and that the jammed rifle was the only thing that had stopped him. They were in the midst of battle and taking the Syrian hostage wasn't possible under the circumstances, and still Amos considered having mercy on him. This all took place within a fraction of a second, and then the Syrian reached for his vest to pull out a grenade, and Amos shot a long barrage that sliced through the man's body from top to bottom. Everything spilled out. Amos, whose face or voice I could not recall, said he'd turned around, walked away, puked his guts out, and resumed fighting. The entire box was filled with these voices.

*

After I'd been discharged, I got an ugly rash on my fingers. I thought it would go away on its own, but it only got worse. I got these disgusting warts, which to this day, some years later, I haven't been able to get rid of. It upset me because I'd always paid attention to people's hands, how groomed and aesthetic they were. I viewed the state of a person's fingernails and the wholeness of their skin as a symbol of their emotional state and despised people with neglected hands. And now I had to hide my own hands, covering them with Band-Aids, and I was ashamed. I went to see a dermatologist, who recommended a cream, and when the cream didn't help I went to see another doctor to get a second opinion. There was a waiting list to get an appointment, so I paid out of pocket to see her sooner. She tried to burn one of my fingers with oxygen. It hurt and only made things worse. Finally, I went to see the most prestigious professor in town, and after he looked at my fingers and hummed something to himself, he asked if I'd been under pressure recently. After thirty-five years in the field, he knew how to recognize stress-induced skin conditions, he said, and this was one of them.

"I'm not under any particular sort of pressure," I told him, "but my life isn't exactly nirvana either."

He asked what I did for a living, and when I told him I was a psychologist he smiled widely and was kind enough to spare me the famous saying about the cobbler's shoes that had holes in them, though I could tell it was on the tip of his tongue. "Don't do dishes or mop the floor, avoid getting your hands wet, keep using that cream you were given, but most importantly, try to keep calm, and then it might go away," he concluded, sending me away.

I thought of going to rest up at Mandy's, but my date-book was full of appointments and I couldn't abandon my patients because of some frivolous skin condition. I had learned from Dad never to cancel an appointment, that it was my duty to rise above my human weaknesses, that the show must go on. Even when he was burning with fever and Mom begged him to take a day or two off work, he would just drink a cup of tea with lemon and honey, take some meds, and continue to see his patients as usual. He would always dress up for them, donning tailor-made silk shirts and a British jacket, a pair of pants that Mom had ironed flawlessly, and polished leather shoes. He never shared his problems with his patients. When he sat with them, he was like a god descended from heaven. That's what I'd learned from him—we were a wall for them to hurl their problems against, he said, and we must never fall apart.

"What's on your fingers?" Dad asked the first time he saw my warts.

"Nothing," I said, closing my hands into fists. "Nothing. I went to see a few doctors. It's hard to get rid of."

When I was eleven years old, Mom had bought me my first deodorant and taught me how to remove the hair from my legs and armpits. When I protested, she'd said I should talk to Dad, because he was the one who said it was time.

"Your body is crying for help," Dad said now, amused.

"Can you cure me, Dad?" I asked, feigning a childish voice just to aggravate him.

"If you give me a few years, yes," he said. "But I don't think I've got a few years left. Besides, in this post-Freudian world, it's no longer customary for an analyst to treat his own children. Your fingers want to touch—a man, the land, life. But you let them down. You run away, always staying behind, allowing others to touch, to live life instead of you."

"Cut it out, Dad."

"I won't. I only want what's good for you. Your fingers and I have known you ever since you were born. I'm giving words to what your fingers are trying to say. This is a final warning for passengers on the wrong train to switch lines—"

"Dad, I do exactly what you do," I cut him off. "I treat people. Isn't that good enough for you?"

"You don't treat people," he said calmly, facing me with his heavy, grave features, which I loved so much and feared so terribly. "You are a servant of power, and that's fine. People have built grand careers out of that. But you're on the margins. Others kill, others screw, others conquer, and you stand on the sidelines, offering advice, and you think it makes a difference. It pains me just like it pains your fingers, because I remember what a gifted child you used to be. The whole world was open to you."

"Do you have any idea what kind of poor souls I treat, Dad? How many lives I try to save?" I asked, trying hard not to cry. "Or the price I pay in order to hear them out, hold their experiences, and process their traumas? What do you even know about me, Dad?"

He was unshaken. Dad never apologized or showed remorse. He said, "That's admirable, of course, but it's pointless, because you yourself are a part of this machine, which continues to breed more and more misery. If you killed people yourself, you'd at least gain some satisfaction from it, but you don't even have that. This is what your fingers are saying, I'm just translating for them. But"—he placed his hand on my wrist, and I didn't shake it off—"not all is lost. You're still fairly young. That's your major advantage over me. Don't think I have no regrets. Ultimately, I've left no mark on the world, nor will I. But you still have a chance. The day these lesions on your hands heal, you'll know you're headed in the right direction."

7

ALL OF ISRAEL'S FIGHTS and tragedies—the battles, the run-ins, the training accidents, the terrorist attacks—were relived in my clinics, three days a week, six sessions a day, forty-five minutes a session. Sometimes survivors came to me strung out on psychiatric medication. You could tell these patients were disturbed right away. Other times, I saw functioning people whose secret was known to none but their family. Sometimes they were able to hide their disability even from those closest to them, only revealing the scars at my clinic.

Nivi was one of my more complicated patients. He was almost forty years old and still lived with his mother. She drove him to our sessions and I made an exception, allowing her to wait in my kitchen while he and I sat in the clinic. We were having our fourth session, and once again he told me the story of the run-in, the one I knew by heart at that point, a version from which he never veered.

How they walked in a row down an alleyway, how their officer made a navigation mistake and turned someplace they shouldn't have gone, where they were surprised by a mob hurling rocks, bottles, and iron at them.

"They hated me. They wanted to break me into atoms, to gouge my eyes out," Nivi told me, always using the same words, starting to pace restlessly around the room.

"Sit down, Nivi," I said. "Have some water. You're here. You're safe."

He sat down on the edge of the chair, then got right back up again. "They approached us with knives. They wanted to cut me," he said, demonstrating with his hands. "All of a sudden I saw the guy ahead of me in the row falling down. Someone dropped a construction block on him from above. His skull shattered. I could tell he was dead right away. Then someone on our side opened fire. There was no choice. I didn't shoot. I couldn't, my hands were shaking, I just wanted to get out of there. We started to back out of the alley, carrying our friend with us. I grabbed his legs. When we got to the main street they shouted, *Get in the car already, get in*. They were yelling at me, but I couldn't move. It was as if I wanted to let the Arabs get me, like I was tired of this life. Then one guy came at me, trying to butcher me with an enormous knife that glinted in the sun and blinded me, and my friend shot him in the head and saved my life. Everything spilled out, his brain spraying in all directions. He was still standing, the Arab, a headless man with a knife in his hand. *Get in, get in!* they shouted and pulled me into the car, and the Arabs were screaming, and—" He was standing in the middle of my clinic, yelling, in the heart of horror, and I was getting worried, because we'd lost touch with each other. I was no longer in control of this situation. Nivi was now controlled by the most ancient, most primitive parts of his brain, and there was no room for his rational mind.

His mother rushed over from the kitchen, banging on the clinic door, worried he might try to hurt me. But she couldn't help me now.

"Go," I told her from behind the door. A cowardly therapist would leave the room and call the police, but that would be a betrayal of my patient, like fleeing a battlefield. Instead, I waited for him to grow tired of yelling and of the bizarre twitches that went with it; for his brain to recover from being flooded. There, it was happening, Nivi was tiring out, his head plopping down.

"Sit down, Nivi," I said gently. "Everything's okay, we're not there."

He looked at me vaguely, letting out a cry of pain, and that's when I was finally able to put a hand on his shoulder. He curled into me. I held him for a moment, smoothing out the rug he'd wrinkled when he stamped his feet.

"I didn't touch you, I didn't hit you, I didn't touch you," he said, shriveled into the armchair. His rational mind was turning on again, and I assured him that everything was fine. He didn't hurt me.

"How do you feel?"

"Exhausted," he said. "I'm so tired of this. It's like this every time, and after it happens, I can't do anything else. The kids in the building are scared of me. Their parents hold them close when they see me in the stairwell. They look at me like I'm a monster. But I've never touched them. I don't hit them. I've got nothing against children. I try to explain to people that I'm the only one I kill, but that doesn't reassure them."

When his mother first brought him in, she told me he'd been to dozens of doctors and had been hospitalized a few times, with no improvement. She'd heard wonderful things about me and believed I was the only one who could save him. She begged me to take him on. But even after several sessions, Nivi remained trapped in the traumatic event, and I'd had no luck in pulling him out of there. I wondered how Dad would treat him. Whenever I got stuck with a patient I asked myself if Dad would have done any better. Perhaps his classic, slow, and patient method would have built a sturdier bridge. Perhaps he would have detected a doorway into Nivi's mind that I'd missed.

Nivi was calm now. I was handing him a tissue to wipe the sweat from his face when he suddenly asked, "You remember when you visited our battalion during training, before anything happened, when I was still okay?"

I tensed. This was the end of our fourth session, and it was the first time he'd mentioned that meeting.

"Of course I remember," I said. "I'd just started on the job and I wanted to see you on the field."

Nivi chuckled and said, "They told us a psychologist was coming and that we'd better behave. We were a little concerned, but when you showed up you were really sweet, not at all frightening. We liked you. I remember you went out on our training with us and someone let you shoot a few machine-gun barrages. We were so impressed. That was when we realized you were on our side and that you came to work with us, not to watch us like animals at the zoo."

I blushed. I couldn't help it.

Nivi smiled. He now looked like a normal guy who'd managed to get a girl's attention. He carried on. "Then, at night, we heard you sitting with the officers outside Rosolio's tent and we all thought something was going to happen between you two. You guys really clicked. Actually, we all had thoughts about you. You know how young soldiers are. We liked you. We talked about you."

"Ancient history. Well, it's nice to hear anyway." I smiled awkwardly and wondered when he would bring up the other, more problematic encounter we'd had the night before the battle. "That's a good place for us to pick up again at our next session," I added. It had already been forty-five minutes, and we had to finish. His mother was waiting outside the door. When I opened it, I told her we'd had a rough start but that he'd settled down and we'd made a bit of progress.

"I thought you might need some help," she said. Weighing over two hundred pounds, Nivi stood before her, his head lowered, like a scolded child.

"Let's go," she said, taking his hand. "Thank you, doctor," she murmured, shoving some bills into my hand. "See you next week."

After they left, I opened the door between the clinic and the rest of the apartment and sat down in the living room, in front of the window overlooking the street. There was a tree there whose branches shifted slowly in the wind. I needed to breathe.

*

I was sitting at a high viewpoint, underneath a tarp, the unit commander by my side. The boys were running and crawling beneath us in the scorching sun. We watched them through binoculars. I was taking notes. They thought I was observant, a wizard, a prophetess who could predict which of them would make a good commando warrior, so they continued to invite me to these tryout days, treating me like a queen.

A few hundred virile young men disembarked from buses early in the morning, receiving gear, eager to prove themselves. The energy pouring out of them was enough to move a continent. Their shirts were marked with numbers so we could recognize them. First, they were made to jog a few miles so as to eliminate the weakest, the ones who'd ended up here by mistake. About a third were eliminated right away or dropped out willingly. The others were bombarded with tasks: crawl through the sand, carry heavy sacks, dig holes. Their physical prowess and endurance were tested, and after every round of tasks, the young officers circling them said through a loudspeaker, "Anyone who's having too much trouble can leave." A few young men dragged their feet away, heads lowered, giving up their alpha male dreams. Perhaps later in life they would find professional success, be exemplary citizens or family men, but this moment of failure would leave a scar. The remaining—the strong—were made to run in circles before us, carrying gurneys loaded with heavy sandbags, as we waited to see how many of them broke. Occasionally the testers shoved them or set obstacles in their path, teasing them to gauge their response—would they lose their cool or keep their eyes on the prize in spite of the intense physical duress? I was asked whether I thought the officers ought to shoot bullets over their heads, as the military used to do but had now curtailed for safety reasons. I was told it was necessary in order to test their basic fitness for battle conditions. In the past, I would have said no. We don't do that kind of thing. It could break their spirits. But now I thought we ought to be tougher on them, and recalled my most recent conversation with Rosolio. Their clothes were drenched with sweat, their bodies beaten and aching, they were running through the sand carrying a heavy weight when suddenly they were stopped in order to practice crossing a thick barbed wire fence laid across the ground. I was sitting above, assessing their levels of fatigue, stress, and breaking points, like an engineer of the soul.

"See this sand hill?" the officer asked through the loudspeaker. "Charge it. But each and every one of you has to make it to the top. If one of you stays behind, you all fail."

The group was smaller now, many having defected, and some of those remaining looked wiped out and desperate. The testers sent them away with the point of a finger and a brief statement. I looked among them for the strong and the determined, those who wouldn't give up. They were recognizable by their confident posture and the decisiveness of their movements; by the way others instinctively lined up behind them. They were the leaders of the pack. Had there been any females around, they would be drawn to these men. Once, Shauli and I had visited a deer sanctuary in the Galilee. We had watched how the dominant males controlled all the others—the young, the elderly, the weak, and most of all, the females.

The testers stood in the middle of the incline the young men were charging, blocking their path, pushing them down. The testers were light-limbed, strong, and authoritative, and the recruits were not allowed to push them back. Their brains and willpower had to take precedence over their exhausted muscles. Time and again they tried to reach the top, only to be shoved back down. The strong could make it, but they'd been tasked with leading the others up there as well. I liked these games. I designed some of them myself, and each time I watched them, mesmerized, from my spot on the top of the hill.

In the afternoon, a short list of serious candidates remained. The others had already been sent home on buses. Through the binoculars, I saw one of the eliminated boys, destroyed with disappointment. *We just saved your life*, I told him silently. *You wouldn't have been able to take it, and in the moment of truth, your weakness would have put others at risk.*

We tested them like this for three days. Each part of the day had a defined purpose marked with numbers and tables. We woke them up in the middle of the night from the deepest sleep to head out on a stretcher-carrying hike. The tester roused them with loud cries: "Anyone who wants to keep sleeping is welcome to. Sweet dreams. You'll be on the bus home tomorrow morning." One or two were tempted to drop out that way, staying curled up in their sleeping bags. This was how we discovered which of them broke under the pressure of exhaustion and pain. A lack of perseverance. Despair. Fear. And which of them could continue to rely on their brains even as their bodies cried for help. Which of them faked it. And which could give up their personal comfort for the sake of others, a born leader. At the end of the third day, only twenty-five candidates remained, who were brought to me for interviews. They were given sandwiches, which they ate quickly before being led up the hill to the tarp, under which I sat with the special-unit commander. I had in front of me the results of their tests. I'd watched them perform like gladiators in the arena for three days. I knew that anyone who made it this far was strong and talented, but I had to make sure that none of them was disturbed or megalomaniacal; that they did not suffer any yet undiscovered personality disorders. I listened to their voices and enunciations, examined their expressions and body language. After twenty-five years in the business, a short conversation was sufficient for me to reach a diagnosis. That's why I was asked to come back again and again.

They sat across from me, tense. I was the final task they had to endure. I wore a silk blouse, the top button undone, smelling fresh with the slightest hint of perfume, my hair in a bun, reading glasses on the tip of my nose. I could be their mother, and yet, even after they'd crawled through the hot sand for three days, I sometimes detected a twinkle in their eyes—*Maybe you and I can get together sometime in a different life*.

"Tell me about a low point you've experienced," I instructed them. "And about a high point, a great joy you experienced." Then I processed the signals their voices and gesticulations delivered. Most of them discussed the death of a loved one or failing an important exam, and I delved a little deeper, checking to see if sadness was chronic for them, if they might break following a failure or if one of their friends died in battle. I tested their high points too—could they restrain joy, or would they get carried away and lose control after every victory? I asked them about their hobbies. "Tell me about your family. Your parents, your siblings." I sought out the tiny twitches, checking eye contact. "Tell me about your friends. How much do you love them?" We weren't interested in any lone wolves, but we didn't want the kind of people who needed constant approval. "Have you ever felt despair?" Most of them said no, and I believed them. Those who'd made it this far were not the despairing kind. But if I picked up on any signs of lying I continued digging until I reached the truth. "Do you have a girlfriend?" I asked. Some of them did, and were already apparently trained in the masculine skill of talking to women. Others smiled bashfully. I saw their pimples, a belated childhood erupting from them, and I wanted to cross to the other side of the field desk and bury their heads in my lap.

A few weeks after our initial meeting at the Chief of Staff chambers, Rosolio called me in again. This time he'd convened a large forum of major generals and brigadier generals, which he titled the Victory Workshop. The goal was to come up with a plan for returning to the glory days when our victories at war were crushing and unequivocal.

"In spite of our immense advantage in every possible parameter," Rosolio said at the start of the meeting, "every one of our recent operations has ended in more or less a tie. The enemy was not defeated, not brought to their knees. Instead of a victory cry, we were left with the foul taste of compromise. My intention is to achieve a decisive victory in the next war, and that's why I've asked you all here."

He'd asked me to sit on the sidelines and watch, then give him my thoughts. He introduced me to the higher-ups: *This is Abigail, lieutenant colonel in reserve duty, formerly the head of behavioral sciences, paratrooper mental health officer, etc.* Some of the officers were already familiar with me, and to others I was a stranger. As usual, I had to submit to their cruel scrutiny, as if I were modeling swimsuits. Not that I cared. The only thing that bothered me was the Band-Aids on my right-hand fingers. I was embarrassed by them. I wanted my whole, pretty fingers back.

One of the high points of my collaboration with Rosolio had been the reoccupation of Nablus, sending his brigade to conquer the city and clear it of the terrorist hubs that launched suicide bombers into Israeli cities. I accompanied him personally. To be less modest, it would be more accurate to say that I had mentally prepared him for the mission. Rosolio had been concerned. He had rich experience in specific commando operations, but this was the first large-scale brigade mission he'd commanded. The night before the operation commenced, when the two of us were alone in his office, he told me about his fear of failure.

"I'm having a hard time looking my soldiers in the eyes," he said. "I know some of them won't survive because of me, because of mistakes and bad decisions I'll make. The command center asked me to estimate the number of casualties we'll suffer, but I won't play that game. I want everyone to come home alive. Otherwise, I'm the one who's going to have to go see their mothers and explain myself to them. Nobody else."

This wasn't a good starting point. I only had a short time to treat him, because early the next morning the soldiers would all gather to receive his orders before heading out to battle, and it would be a disaster if he spoke to them with such hesitation. He was tired and stressed, but I couldn't touch him. There were photos of his wife and daughters on the wall behind him. I didn't have the courage yet. My role was to alleviate his concerns and reinforce his confidence so he could make the necessary sacrifices. You cannot be a military leader without leading people to their deaths. His desire to bring all soldiers home alive was unrealistic. I steered him gently. He didn't require a whip, but a wise, decisive caress. Though his personality was strong and well-developed, it cracked under pressure, and I could hear the fragmentation and had to stop it.

I made us strong, sweet tea and led him out of the office, into the summer night. We spoke softly and up close. From a distance, one might have mistaken us for a pair of lovers. I asked who else, besides his soldiers, he envisioned right now. He spoke about his wife and daughters, who were still young, asleep at home. I asked him to describe his little girls' lives, their schedule, their meals and baths and games, their bedroom. Then I asked him to describe them twenty years from now, as young women. What hopes did he have for them? I didn't even mention war. He softened, smiled, and relaxed. I wanted to touch him, to kiss him, to take him to his room, but I drew a curtain over my desire. I had to sharpen his sword with words until it shone. We talked about his daughters, about his favorite places, about everything but me. Gradually, I directed the conversation back to the military. I asked him to describe himself as a young soldier and a junior officer. What did he remember from those days?

"I was very skinny," he laughed. "Thin and light and strong. I sometimes think about the things I used to do and am impressed with myself. Where did I get the guts or intelligence to do them? Everything was new to me. The rifle was new, the maps were new, and the places I went, and the authority I held. And I was naive . . . as naive as my soldiers. That's why I want so badly to protect them. I look at these soldiers, and they're like my little brothers. They're me twenty years ago. I can't bring them back to their parents dead."

"But Rani," I said, moving closer and speaking into his darkened face, "when you were their age you didn't think of yourself as a boy. You didn't feel like a boy. You trusted yourself. You were wise and strong. You were pissed off at anyone who looked down at you."

"That's true," said Rosolio. "You're right." And a beautiful thing happened before my eyes, like a rare natural phenomenon: the worry and hesitation on his face were replaced with intelligent, self-possessed sturdiness. It was a therapeutic moment I'll never forget: I'd drained out the pus of doubt and fear with the scalpel of my words, and now he was clean.

The next morning, Rosolio faced his soldiers, spread out before him in the formation quad, and gave them the speech we'd composed together the previous night, before I sent him to bed. We'd inserted all the right messages, planting them into the text one by one, and he recited them with utter, persuasive confidence that emerged from the bottom of his heart. I could see on the soldiers' faces that they were captivated. When he reached the climax of his speech they groaned and purred like trained animals about to be set loose on the hunt, like the armies of a Roman warlord.

Almost twenty years had gone by, and now I was sitting at the corner of a conference desk and at the head was Rosolio, Chief of Staff. I took notes in my pad about the other participants, Rosolio's generals, whose job it was to deliver this victory to him: Weak. Hesitant. Chatty. Kind of impressive. Decisive. Smart. Not deep. Unripe, needs more work. Pompous. The entire arc of human qualities was listed in my notes. Occasionally, Rosolio's eyes twinkled at me. I was the only person in the room who was close with him. They were chatting way too much for soldiers. It's hard to win with such an excess of words. Rosolio barely spoke. He was wracking his brain trying to figure out how to shake up these people and turn them into wild horses. Most of them looked like the VPs of midsize companies, I thought, who'd settled down in a little home outside of town with a jeep and a pretty wife and were satisfied. Why spoil a good thing with the hell of war? We had taken away their wreaths and prizes, the young female soldiers and public admiration, limited their maneuvering territory, encumbered them with lawyers. They weren't even allowed to smoke. They were neutered. Was it any surprise they were limping away with their heads hanging like donkeys rather than striding ahead like noble steeds?

After the forum was dispersed, I was left alone with Rosolio in his chambers.

"What do you think about them?" he asked.

I was familiar with that look of his, and he was familiar with mine. There was no need for me to answer. "Go see the soldiers, Rani," I told him. "Be with them, talk to them, let them see you, let them hear you. The people I saw in here won't do the job for you. Go to the young officers, the ones who aren't yet jaded. Those are the people you ought to work with. They're the ones you'll be able to imbue with a fighting spirit."

"I guess I don't have any other choice," he said glumly.

"Are you planning a war soon?" I asked.

"Maybe. And when it happens, I plan on winning, even if I have to lead the forces in myself."

"I'd be happy to help you," I said. I was certain he remembered that monumental late-night conversation, years ago, when I'd saved him from himself.

I saw him hesitating, biting his lips, but he said, "I asked about your son today. I was told he's doing just fine."

"Why did you ask about him?" I said, startled.

"I was talking to the brigade commander when I remembered he had your kid in basic training. I didn't tell him anything, don't worry. I just said I've known him since he was born. I didn't ask for any special treatment. The brigade commander asked his direct supervisors and reported back that he's a good soldier, a good friend, that they're pleased with him. You raised him well, Abigail. You should be very proud of yourself."

I was so angry. He'd broken our deal. But we were in the Chief of Staff chambers and I couldn't cause a scene. Yet to be honest, the compliment touched my heart and bloated my ego.

It was only when I walked out of base that I made the connection between this war Rosolio was planning and Shauli. You fool, I thought. What are you doing?

8

COME TO THE BEACH, Noga texted.

"Are you alone there?" I asked.

"Totally," she wrote back. It was Thursday afternoon, early summer, and she'd just come to town from the squadron for a long weekend.

I hadn't been to the beach in forever, even though I lived only a fifteen-minute walk away. When Shauli was little we used to go almost every Saturday and spent many happy hours there. It's too short notice, I thought. I'm not beach-ready. I wasn't sure my old bathing suit still fit, and even if it did, it certainly wasn't in style. And I hadn't had a wax in a long time. But Noga was waiting for me. I put on a one-piece that looked awful and covered it up with an old beach wrap I'd bought during some forgettable vacation, strapped on a pair of ugly sandals, glanced in the mirror, and changed everything for another set of rags, then forced myself to head out the door before I could change my mind, before she got away.

I recognized her from behind as I walked onto the sand. She was sitting alone on a wide blanket, wearing a dark bikini, looking peacefully at the sea.

"Noga," I called.

She turned around and shot me a honey smile like a gorgeous actor in some old Italian ad. "I thought you weren't going to make it. The sun's going to set soon," she said, making some room for me beside her. A few guys were sitting not too far from us, staring at her. I was like the evil aunt who'd come to chaperone. I took a seat, embarrassed by her exposed body, trying to look only at her face. I kept my cover on, and Noga asked if I'd brought a swimsuit and if I felt like getting in the water.

"Isn't it too cold?" I asked.

She laughed and said it was only the Mediterranean Sea, and it was already summer. Some people swam in it all winter long. She explained it to me like I was a tourist, as if I hadn't known this beach since I was a little girl.

I took off my old *sharwal*. "I bought it in Sinai a billion years ago," I apologized.

Noga smiled. "Let's go," she said, "to the water!"

She ran into the sea, dove in, and rowed her arms, her elbows bending and straightening as her fingers connected with the water, her arms and shoulders painted sunset gold. I got stuck ankle-deep. I was cold and wanted to go back, but she called out to me to get in, to stop worrying. I couldn't back down now. On three, I told myself and rushed in. A few seconds later, I was already used to the water. We swam side by side toward the breakwater, away from the other bathers, where we rested for a spell, submerged up to our necks, kicking our feet.

"This is where Shauli surfs," I told her. "He spends all summer here."

Noga said that since she didn't grow up near the beach she never learned to properly surf, but that now she'd really like to. She always said things matter-of-factly like that, clean, devoid of any effeminate gossip, as if she were a resourceful, athletic young boy. Had she not broken down during captivity training, I might have mistakenly thought she was made of ice. We didn't have much to say to each other outside of the clinic. She was so young. All I wanted was to be around her.

We got out of the water. I'd forgotten to bring a towel and was shivering, my teeth chattering. She offered me her towel and I insisted that she use it first, until finally we found ourselves sharing it, giggling. We were exposed to the world, and I didn't care.

"Want to come see my apartment?" she asked as we rinsed our feet in the spigot. Her toes were narrow and long, her nails clean and healthy, without any polish.

"Sure," I said, embarrassed by my own enthusiasm.

We walked back with wet clothes and wild hair. Noga said I looked like I'd been electrocuted, and when I came across my reflection in a store window I started to laugh. The city looked new through her eyes, the familiar landscape turning special and beautiful, and I felt young. We stopped at the greengrocer. Noga was in the mood for fruit. She picked out early-season grapes and apricots and we nearly finished them on the walk back.

She lived in a shabby apartment on one of the side streets sloping down to the beach, but the rooms were spacious and the ceiling was high, like they used to build them. She invited me into her bedroom, which was nearly empty, save for a hard, low bed and a small bookcase with a few books and some felt dolls her grandmother had made her when she was little. "I haven't had a chance to hang up any pictures," she apologized, and I told her I thought it looked nice like this. The other bedroom belonged to her roommate, who was at work.

"Go ahead and shower," Noga said, handing me a clean towel.

I asked if she could lend me a shirt and pants.

"Of course," she said, and added some simple cotton underwear.

I stood under the hot water in this unfamiliar shower for a long time, testing Noga and her roommate's fragrant products—maybe I'd find some potion of eternal youth—until I felt the hot water running out. I walked out of the bathroom wearing Noga's clothes, a towel wrapped around my head. "I think I finished your hot water," I apologized.

She said it was no big deal, she'd just rinse off.

While Noga showered, I sat on the edge of her bed and examined the photos on the rattan shelves: a picture of her parents, who were handsome and fit, and one of Noga with her younger brother and sister. I thought about the grandiosity of a true family, unlike the miniature one I'd created for Shauli and me. I didn't leave the room when she came back from the bathroom, wrapped in a towel. She got dressed behind the closet door and I saw nothing save for her pretty calves, which rose and fell as she pulled on her underwear and shorts.

"Look, we're dressed the same!" she cheered as she revealed herself to me.

We sat in the small kitchen and she insisted on cooking us pasta with tomato sauce, even though I told her not to go to any trouble. She caught me watching her as she cooked, smiled bashfully, and said, "What?"

"Nothing," I said. I was charmed by every little thing she did.

When we sat down to eat she told me she felt as if the chopper had become a part of her body. At first it was a foreign machine made out of metal, but now she thought of it as a flying horse, like the real horses she rode back in her village, responding to her every move. The only difference was she couldn't give the chopper a sugar cube.

"That's great," I said. "We've been waiting for years for a girl to do this job, and now—" I wasn't sure why I'd switched to first person plural, and who exactly I was speaking for.

"I don't think about that," she said, cutting me off. "When I'm up there I don't even think of myself as a woman. I only think of the job I have to do and the fun of flying."

"You're absolutely right," I said. It would be a shame to spoil this unique kind of fun. We sat in the kitchen next to the old, rattling fridge, she blew on the tea she'd made after we finished eating and put the cup to her lips. I drank too and felt my body relax. This was enough. There was no need to want anything more.

*

One afternoon, many years earlier, Mom had walked into my bedroom and closed the door quietly behind her. I was studying for the GED, and Dad was seeing a patient in the clinic. It was a rare occasion. We didn't share that kind of intimacy, and she typically respected my privacy. Our conversations were shallow, focusing on everyday minutiae. I didn't respect her. She wasn't smart and important like Dad, so I never tried to impress her. I couldn't figure out the quiet, unambitious manner with which she'd chosen to live her life. When I was diagnosed as gifted in the third grade she'd objected to the idea of transferring me into a special class at a different school; Dad was the one who ultimately made the call to go ahead with the switch. In my childish brain, I thought she wanted me to be regular, like her. I was convinced she envied me, and I'd been wary of her ever since, lest she poison the shining future I had in store. She recoiled from me as well.

"May I?" she asked before sitting on my bed. I nodded and kept poring over textbooks at my desk. "Come sit next to me," she pleaded. "I don't like you towering over me like that."

I got off the chair and went to sit beside her. She was wearing a dress and her legs were plump and pretty. A few hours earlier, I had announced to my parents that I'd enrolled in the military academic program, in psychology studies. It came as an utter surprise, and I knew that's what she wanted to talk about.

"You're not a regular child, Abigail," my mother said in a formal, unnatural tone, meant to cover up her insecurity. "We could tell almost from the moment you were born. You started talking before you were even a year old. If it were up to your father, you'd have started college a long time ago. He'd have you skip as many grades as possible. But I did my best to let you have a normal childhood, to let you have friends, go to dance class, enjoy free time, grow up the right way. I think I was right, even though I know you don't value my opinion much. What I wanted to tell you, Abigail, is that it's too early for you to lose yourself in these affairs of the mind. You won't have a normal life if you get into all that now. You still need to develop, to grow emotionally, to get to know people. I'm asking you, Abigail, to reconsider. Go do regular military service like everyone else. With your mind, you're sure to land an interesting role, meet a great guy who falls in love with you, and then decide what you want to do with your life, when you're older. Not now."

I looked at her with arrogant insult. I thought she was trying to hinder my path. "What's a normal life, Mom? Being like you? Like your friends?"

"Don't condescend, Abigail," Mom said, her face twisting. "My friends and I started families, studied. We work, perhaps not in the most heroic professions, but we built ourselves a life. You haven't done any of that yet." She meant I hadn't slept with a man. That's how I interpreted her words. That was my point of weakness. I looked at her legs, which had given Dad pleasure, and I couldn't compete with them.

"And what if I don't get married, Mom? Would that mean I'm not normal?"

"I think you'd be sad," she said, her eyes turning from hostility to hurt. "Life with your father isn't easy, but he fills my world. Living alone is very cold and lonely."

"I'll think about it, Mom," I lied. I wasn't about to put any thought into her advice. I was determined and didn't understand what she was trying to tell me. She was younger than I am now, tan and attractive, and all I wanted was for her to get out. Her proximity weighed heavily on me.

When Shauli was born, years later, Mom took devoted care of him night and day, while I was busy with my career. I thought the world would veer off course if I let go. Mom never demanded gratitude or asked for anything in return. But we didn't grow any closer then, either. Our conversations were technical.

We coordinated schedules and exchanged vital information about Shauli's meals and bowel movements.

A few days before she died, when she was already very sick, I sat with her in their living room, whispering so as not to disturb Dad. "Do you remember the conversation we had that day you came into my room?" I asked her.

She was shriveled, smiling in pain. "It's lucky you didn't take my advice," she said. "You were always smarter than I was. And stronger. I'm proud of you. You forged your own path."

"I'm not so sure, Mom," I said, taking her emaciated hand with its bulging veins.

"No, no, you're wonderful," she insisted in a whisper. "Look at your success, how everyone admires you. And you've got a terrific child. You did it all. And you did it your own way."

"Thanks, Mom." I smiled. I didn't want to sadden her with my tales of lonesomeness and sorrow. It was too late for that.

I called Noga on Saturday night. I couldn't help myself. I told her I had a lot of fun at the beach and asked if there was any chance of getting together again that night. I could hear she was in a crowded place. Some guy was talking right next to her and there was lots of whooping and hollering. I pictured her drinking and laughing, away from my gloomy disposition. It was so loud she couldn't hear what I said. I hung up and texted her that I was looking forward to our next beach excursion. She texted back a smiley face and a parasol emoji.

9

I SHOWED MY YOUNG BATTALION commanders the black-and-white film of the famous experiment conducted by Dr. Stanley Milgram at Yale in 1961. He demonstrated the way regular people, randomly chosen, could be made to obey orders to give dangerous electric shocks to others. The test subjects were brought into a lab, where they were greeted by a scientist in a white robe with an authoritative appearance and tone of voice. They were seated beside a switch, facing another person on the other side of the glass, who was connected to the electrical current. This other person was referred to as a student, and whenever they answered a question wrong, they were punished with an electric shock. The scientist ordered test subjects to gradually increase the intensity of the current, until it reached a lethal degree. Whenever they showed signs of hesitation, he said they had to obey and not to worry, that he would bear all responsibility. The students were actors who were not truly being electrocuted, but the test subjects were convinced it was all real.

"That's how it works, folks," I said. "Consciousness is a pretty simple instrument. The greater your authority, the more persuasive, the closer you are to your soldiers, the more they'll obey you and the more efficiently they'll kill. If you're far away from them in some war room, giving orders from a distance, it'll be easier for them to evade you. You have to be assertive. If you're weak or hesitant, they won't listen to you. No normal person likes to kill. That's what you're there for, that's what your ranks are for—to make them kill. Pay attention to what happens in Milgram's experiment: whenever the actor cries with pain, the test subjects hesitate. They don't know what to do. When this happens in a military situation, that's exactly when you need to step in like the scientist in the white coat, saying, *Don't worry, this is on me, turn up the intensity*. Thus assuming all moral responsibility. It isn't enough for you to order your soldiers to kill. You have to release them from their scruples. The state, the leaders, the flag, the anthem, all those accessories that justify killing—they come later. You guys are your soldiers' emotional life vest. Without you, they're nothing but murderers."

They shifted uncomfortably in their seats.

"What you're telling us is very problematic," the artillery officer who liked to argue said. "Our soldiers are operating out of a value system, not blindly following orders. They're certainly not murderers. I'm offended by that word."

"I've yet to see a single soldier rely on their value system in battle," I answered bluntly. "In battle, we are controlled by fear, hate, and loyalty to our friends. Values are for civics class in high school, but here we're having an adult conversation. And I never said our soldiers are murderers, God forbid. On the contrary, I'm explaining what distinguishes killing in battle from murder."

"So what," another officer in the back interjected, "are we all just Nazis to you, blindly following orders?"

That angered me. I raised my voice. "Who said anything about Nazis? I'm teaching you how to be better commanders. I'm talking about eliminating enemies, terrorists, people who deserve to die. Why are you bringing Nazis into this?"

They looked at me doubtfully, eyes narrowed. They thought they were unique, that the simple rules that control the lives of all humans didn't apply to them.

"You're turning us into manipulators," said one major with fashionably layered hair, too coifed for a military man. "You're making us into bad people." A small racket ensued, but I knew I could quash it right away.

119

"I've got news for you," I said. "You *are* manipulating them. You're taking eighteen-year-old kids and turning them into soldiers through rituals, symbols, punishments, and all sorts of other enslaving techniques, taking advantage of their desire to be real men. You trick them and play with their minds to make them do things they never dreamed of. One of those things is killing. But there's no choice—without these manipulations no military in the world would exist. I'm on your side, guys. Don't get me wrong. You and I are working toward the same goal," I reassured them. *And for Rosolio*, I added to myself, *to help him achieve his victory and glory*.

"What about the black flag?" asked the only female among them, who had been silent until now.

"The black flag is for you," I said. I looked at her. Her face was shockingly serious and intelligent. "A simple soldier can't see it. How many times have you heard of ranking soldiers refusing orders? Almost never. They can't resist authority. They don't know how. You've got to make that decision for them."

Then someone spoke emotionally about patriotism and the love of the land. I said I had nothing against those ideals. On the contrary, I was all for them. I also liked to listen to old homeland folk tunes. But I told him not to be so gullible as to believe they would be enough to urge his soldiers to charge the enemy, or he might find himself alone on the battlefield.

The lecture ended in a dire mood. I should have prepared a joke to lift their spirits, or else pulled up my skirt and shown them my butt. I heard them whispering awkwardly as they walked out of the classroom. Where was the soul, the ideology, the morality? It hurt them when I presented humankind as a simple machine, a marionette. But I didn't care. In the moment of truth, in battle, when the whole world falls apart, I wanted them to remember what I'd told them plainly, without fakery or hypocrisy, and to know how to kill.

Shauli didn't get leave that Saturday, and Noga was on call, so I went to visit Mandy in the countryside. The loquats in his orchard had ripened, and when I arrived I found him on top of a tall ladder, picking fruit from the tree, bees buzzing all around him. He had fig and pomegranate trees, a few citrus trees, and a fairly large olive grove, from what I could recognize through my city-dweller's eyes.

When he came to me for therapy, I asked Mandy why he'd left the city. He told me that he used to go around with other women while he was married. His wife looked the other way for a few years, until finally he slept with his eldest daughter's best friend, who was seventeen, not even out of high school yet. They were found out and it was just too much to bear. His daughter still hadn't forgiven him to this day. She wouldn't even sit shiva with him after her mother died.

"How did your wife react to what you'd done?" I asked.

Mandy said his wife loved him beyond questions of logic or justice, and that after a few months of crying and distress, she told him if he agreed to move away from the city and promise never to sleep with another woman again, she'd stay with him.

"I kept my word," Mandy said. "I haven't touched another woman ever since. We saved ourselves, moving out here. Instead of other women's bodies, I started to discover the land. I knew nothing at first. I had to teach myself everything from scratch. I worked myself mad, farming in the daytime, making art in the evenings. Those were fantastically creative years. Friends from Tel Aviv wanted to visit, but I wouldn't let them."

Mandy told me their daughter refused to move up to the village with them and stayed back in the city with his wife's parents. "I was a monster," he said in therapy. "There is no forgiveness for what I did to my daughter. But her friend was special, and the pleasure I experienced with her was immense. To this day I burn with the thought of getting in my car and going off to look for her. She should be forty years old now."

I helped Mandy pick the loquats, which were very ripe. He said a greengrocer from the nearby town would come pick up the fruit. The guy paid him close to nothing, but it was a shame to let the fruit rot on the tree.

I stayed over. In the middle of the night, Mandy yelled in his sleep. I was never able to cure him of that habit. I shook his shoulders hard and said, "Mandy, wake up!" When he opened his eyes he was still on the edge of the nightmare and didn't recognize me, until finally his eyes relaxed and focused. He said, "Thank God you're here. I'm sorry, Abigail. It's because of them. Fuck them all."

I caressed his rough, wild hair until he fell asleep again, and I stayed awake on my own with the dark. I thought about Shauli covered with a gray woolen blanket, his long lashes protecting his eyes. He often talked in his sleep. One time he cried, "Daddy, Daddy," which angered me, aroused my envy, and made my heart tremble, all at once. The next morning, I didn't dare ask who he'd seen in the dream.

When I got home I pulled up Shauli's bar mitzvah film. For some reason, I needed to see it. I tensed, my pulse quickening, just like it did every time I watched it.

There we were, standing at the entrance to the event hall on a Saturday afternoon. Shauli reached up to my shoulders as he welcomed his guests. We had a small extended family, and in light of the occasion Mom had tracked down every distant cousin she could muster to make sure we didn't have an empty room. One of those anonymous relatives was now talking Shauli's ear off at the door as he listened politely. Poor little boy, he didn't even know her name. Another cousin of mine from some far-off kibbutz passed by in the background. Then I flinched onscreen. A proper family walked into the frame, a father, a mother, and two daughters. Rosolio, his wife, and their beautiful girls. He'd met his wife in the army as well, just like he'd met me. She was an education officer in his battalion, a woman with a kind, steady face. You could see in the film how I wound as tight as a coil as they walked in. I'd invited them, but hadn't really expected them to show up, and now there they were in all their glory, the four of them, outshining all the other guests. I shook the hand of the wife, whom I'd never met before. "Your girls are beautiful," I said. All you could hear on the film was static, but I could read my own lips. She smiled contentedly, and Rosolio fluttered a kiss on my cheeks and held on to my shoulder for a moment. He was already a major general, but that Saturday he wore a nice pair of jeans and a plain, untucked button-down shirt. He looked around, smiling. It was a glimmering moment. And then came a bit I rewound the tape to watch over and over again: Shauli left the anonymous aunt and walked over to greet them. There was a twinkle of recognition in his eyes, a twinkle of curiosity. He nearly sniffed them out like an abandoned cub searching for his long-lost parents and siblings. Rosolio patted his shoulder and said amiably, "I've known your mother for years, from the military." His good little girls stood bashfully to the side. They could sense something too, but couldn't understand it, of course. Only his wife was oblivious. She told me, "This is such a lovely venue you guys chose." I wanted to tell her: *It's just me, I'm the one who chooses, there's nobody but me*. But I resisted the urge. I was very careful. Rosolio and I had a sacred agreement that must never be broken. In the tape, Shauli hadn't grown up yet. His face was smooth, his stature small, and his voice hadn't changed yet. Next to him, Rosolio's beautiful girls looked like brides. I noted the similarity between father and son—in the color of the eyes, the shape of the head, the smile. It was so apparent. I was startled by the thought of one of the other guests commenting on it out loud: *Would you look at how much the bar mitzvah boy looks like the major general? Are the two of you related by any chance?*

Rosolio placed his hand gently on Shauli's back, and Shauli clung to him, seeking his closeness. I turned to the eldest daughter, who was around sixteen years old at the time, a woman physically but still her parents' little girl, and in the meantime a short line of guests formed behind our group. We hadn't invited many people, just over a hundred, but it was lunchtime and everybody was hungry. Rosolio looked very relaxed, fully trusting me. There he was, embracing Shauli, only for a flash, while I stood next to them, overflowing with emotion as my body remained petrified, outwardly behaving like a good little girl. I led them inside to their table. Shauli followed them too, drawn by force of instinct to this family he'd just met, but I ordered him to return to the entrance until the last of the guests arrived. I watched the scene over and over again, pausing on images that contained us together, checking every single detail. That night, after the bar mitzvah celebration was over, Shauli asked me how I'd met Rosolio and what we did together in the military and where they lived and how old the girls were. He practically put me through an interrogation. I answered as best I could, but of course I couldn't tell him the truth.

10

A MILITARY VEHICLE came to drive me to the desert. They had built a new training site there and asked me to take a look and give any notes I had before it became operative.

The driver was listening to a radio station that played unfamiliar songs. They sounded like whiny prayers set to a mellifluous tune. I watched the back of his head and his fingers that drummed against the steering wheel, and amused myself trying to figure out what I was able to learn about him without asking a single question. He caught me watching him through the rearview mirror and I looked away. I wasn't being polite.

The site was surrounded by a tall wall, military and state flags waving in the dry wind. Inside, the team that would be operating the site was waiting for me. They'd built an entire Arab town with a café—low tables and hookahs—a barbershop, a mosque, and market stalls. All around were two- and three-story prefabricated houses, narrow alleyways, and a junkyard, all of which the enemy could use to hide. They'd invested a lot of money in this. Street sounds were played in the background—Arabic chatter, traffic, donkey-drawn carts, muezzin cries, the shouting of peddlers. The walls were adorned with graffiti I wasn't able to read—I'd never bothered to learn Arabic—as well as the portraits of *shahids*.

"Impressive," I said. "You did a good job."

They seated me in the shade, served me Turkish coffee and cookies, and prepared to present me with the image of the enemy, just like they would do to the soldier units who would be coming here soon to train. The facility commander told me the entire team was made up of former combat soldiers who'd been taken off the field for various reasons, and that he'd hand-picked them himself.

"Go," he ordered over the radio, and they popped out of the artificial alleys like toy soldiers on a board game. Some of them wore the enemy's guerrilla uniform. Others wore civilian clothing and carried different weapons—rifles, hand grenades, and knives. They moved from building to building, staging shoot-outs and stakeouts, and occasionally charged at a group playing our Israeli soldiers. I noticed right away how emotionless their choreography was. They were acting technically, without any dramatic flair. I waited patiently for them to finish. I liked the desert air, and the high, clear skies. I didn't mind waiting. Their play lasted nearly thirty minutes. I knew they'd been preparing it for a long time, but it just wasn't right.

"So, what do you say, doctor?" the site commander asked, his large bald head browning in the sun. "We were told you were the top expert in the psychology of battle. What do you think?"

"It just isn't scary," I told him.

The soldiers gathered and sat down beneath us, sweating with effort, staring at me with confusion. They thought they'd done great.

The commander asked me to elaborate. I explained that their job was to inspire terror in the soldiers who train here, in order to immunize their brains and nervous systems against the real thing. "The most difficult thing for a soldier to feel during battle," I said, "is that someone really hates them and wants them dead. It's a paralyzing feeling, like nothing we experience in normal life. Your job is to illustrate this terror to soldiers. Imagine yourselves as tigers pouncing with bared teeth. Watch nature movies, they can teach you a lot. The way a crocodile will erupt out of the water to submerge a stunned gazelle.

Consider the cruelest images possible—chopping off the enemy's balls, removing their tongue, gouging out their eyes. That's what you ought to look like. You need to be their worst nightmare."

They continued to stare at me and I thought, This generation doesn't read anymore, so they don't know how to use their imaginations. That entire part of their brain is distorted.

"Get up," I said, "on your feet."

They stood up languidly. I should have taken a picture of them in that moment and sent it to Rosolio, so he could see who he was dealing with.

"Now," I said, "picture the person you hate the most, someone you'd like to kill, and stab him with your knives. Go on, he's standing right in front of you. I want to see blood in your eyes."

At first they chuckled awkwardly, but then they broke into the murderous knife dance I'd prescribed, their face twisting with hatred, their movements growing sharp and lethal. This was already a significant improvement.

"Excellent," I said, applauding. "That's how you charge, not like robots on tranquilizers."

Now they looked at me appreciatively, beginning to figure out what I wanted from them, and awaiting further instructions.

"Let's practice the reverse scenario," I said. "Imagine you're the enemy, and one of our soldiers takes you by surprise. You aren't prepared, but you're dying to stay alive. Your brain is working overtime, trying to figure out how to make it out alive. You raise your hands, fall to your knees, and beg for mercy. Be humane. Play innocent. Try to trick them."

They split into pairs, soldier and enemy. Some of the enemies tried to shoot and were killed on the spot. The others begged for their lives just as I'd asked them to, and our soldiers pitied them and took them as prisoners.

"Where are you taking them?" I intervened. "You're in the middle of battle. There's no jail, no cable ties. What do you do? Release them so that they can kill you a minute later?"

"So what do you want me to do, shoot someone who just surrendered?" one of the soldiers asked.

"You tell me. I'm just a psychologist. I'm trying to be sensible here."

"If there's no place to put the prisoners and we've got to keep fighting, then I have to kill him," he said hesitantly. "Is that what you're getting at?"

"What do you think?" I asked, ever the professional.

"I think there's no choice, I've got to kill him," he said. And since I gave no response, all the soldiers shot the enemy mercilessly, not even listening to their pleading. Good, I thought, it's their choice.

"You need some women here," I told the commander. I was on a roll. "You've got no children or elderly, no civilian population getting in our soldiers' way, disrupting things, cursing from the balconies, pouring buckets of shit from above, ten-year-olds with rifles, old women carrying explosive devices under their dresses. It's too sterile here, this isn't what war looks like these days."

The commander pulled out a notepad and took down everything I said. I knew I'd given him full value for the money the military had coughed up.

"Do you have any props?" I asked.

"What do you mean?"

"Blood, amputated limbs, spilled guts, rolling heads. Need I say more?" I asked. None of these kids had yet to come close to war; they just didn't get it.

"No," the commander said.

"Then get some!" I shouted. "Everything here is too clean and pretty. There are no demolished walls, no broken windows, no blood puddles. Why am I not hearing kids screaming bloody murder because you just killed their parents? In reality, when battle begins everything turns ugly. Things happen that our brains can't fathom. How do I know? Because I've heard hundreds of stories from soldiers who've been there. This needs to be a horrific place, hell incarnate, and instead it's cute, like Disneyland." I'd given them a proper shakedown and told them I'd be submitting a report of this visit, so they didn't think they could get away with it. Their eyes twinkled with admiration as we said goodbye, as they should have. I'd given them a strong performance.

*

We met every few years, all the kids from the gifted classroom. Most of us still lived in the area, close to our aging parents, like baby birds who'd never been able to fly the nest. Two- or three-year intervals between our get-togethers dulled the shock of witnessing the signs of time etched onto our friends' bodies. This year, we met at Ronnit's apartment, which faced a quiet street and was decorated too colorfully for my taste. Her husband wasn't home. She was an anthropology professor who wore wide, comfy clothes and greeted me warmly. I remembered her being a very sweet child, though we'd never really become friends.

None of us had grown up to become important people, accruing wealth or leaving a mark on the world. The bubble we were raised in never taught us how to fight. We had no urge to sink our teeth or fingernails into what we wanted, refusing to let go, the way less intelligent but much more successful people do. We were fatefully late when we found out that success requires much more than the kind of formal intelligence that can be measured in exams. And yet they were good people, my old friends, contributing members of society. I liked most of them, which was why I attended. I had compassion for them because I hadn't given up yet. One guy, who sat next to me in this most recent get-together, used to be a celebrated math and science genius. He had a sharp mind that I had envied when we were in school together, making me recoil whenever he offered the teacher his brilliant answers. He was handsome, too, while I wasn't all that attractive back then. High school was not my finest moment, and he showed no interest in me. I'd heard he'd gone to America after mandatory military service, where he got a PhD in economics before settling down. A few years ago he suddenly showed up at one of our get-togethers, silver-haired, still handsome. He told us he'd returned to Israel on his own, without his children or his ex-wife, whom he'd divorced long ago. When we asked what he used to do in America, he dropped the names of the large corporations he'd worked for. I googled him later but found few mentions.

He sat down next to me. There were some plates of crudités and quiche on the table, as well as an open bottle of cheap wine. He asked what was new with me. I told him I'd retired from the standing army and was now treating people privately. I didn't feel like sharing anything about my special projects. I asked how he'd been. He said he'd found a job as a financial advisor in an investment management firm. I glanced at his clothes, which had been bought at cheap outlets, his worn-out shoes. To impress me, he told me about his idea for a class action suit, which he was working on with a famous attorney. I took a closer look at him, his lost eyes and prattling mouth, and wondered what the hell this guy had done with his brilliant mind. Where had the spark disappeared to? He had too much to drink for this kind of event and tried to hit on me, decades too late, trusting his still-beautiful face to do the trick. But his breath was foul and the things he said bored me. I had an intimate interest in people only if they bewitched me, and all that was left of him was an empty shell.

People spoke about their children, who served in the military, and I asked where each one was serving—wherever I went, I was still an agent of Rosolio. The responses: Intelligence Corps, Intelligence Corps, Education Corps, a navy land job, and one boy eliminated from a pilot training course. When I told them Shauli was with the paratroopers, the room fell silent.

"*Your* son?" Osnat asked. I never liked her; she was too pretentious. "But he's an only child. How did you let him? Aren't you afraid?"

"No," I said curtly. I didn't want to justify my choices to anyone, didn't want Shauli's name in their mouths. A few of them defended me, saying it was a good thing that some kids still volunteered to join combat units. They were being hypocritical because they were extremely worried about their own children. Then they discussed pointless politics. These conversations bored me; the room was filled with cowardly mediocrity. None of them ever fought for a cause. All they did was complain and wait around for vacations abroad and a painless death. We truly used to be talented children, I remembered it. The adults in our lives had led us to believe we were going to save the world, but had failed to imbue us with a smidgen of healthy selfishness or fighting spirit. I looked around the apartment, the attention paid to making its dwellers comfortable, the gentle marks of the husband and children who were absent. Ronnit, our hostess, who used to be a delicate, smiling child and had remained that way as an adult, walked over to quietly discuss unimportant topics. I played along, chatting, smiling, instructing myself to be forgiving and generous. I was only projecting the disappointment in myself onto them. They'd liberated themselves of the expectations pinned onto us, throwing away the handcuffs. I was the only one who was still restless.

I passed by Noga's apartment on the way home. There was a light on in her roommate's bedroom, but Noga's was dark.

I'm outside your apartment, I texted her. *I just happened to be in the neighborhood.*

Noga texted back a sad face and wrote that she was at the squadron but that she had a plan for the next time we met.

Perhaps I'd go upstairs and knock on the door, ask her roommate for permission to go into Noga's room and splay out on her bed. My place was empty, anyway. Nobody was waiting for me. Instead, I walked into the corner store, bought a beautiful red plum, and sunk my teeth into it. I had to consume something fresh.

Let's go get me a tattoo, Noga texted me on Friday morning.

I was rattled. Why mutilate her flawless body?

Are you coming or not? she texted again. I was already on my way.

We met on the corner near her place and walked over to the tattoo parlor, both of us wearing light sandals. There was a sense of well-being in walking with her. We drew power from each other. We spoke calmly, feeling no need to fill the space between us with a flow of words.

"Why a tattoo?" I asked.

"Because it's pretty," she said.

She's exhibiting her independence, I thought, and let it go. She's still growing.

Sometimes, as we walked, our hands met, and we continued for a spell, holding hands. It wasn't inappropriate. Why would it be? She was like a daughter to me. Her spirits were high because she'd been praised by her commander before leaving base. She'd had a good week. I also felt high, being with her, and the city looked cheerful, colorful, fast.

At the parlor, Noga was handed a catalog. She flipped over to the bird page. She already knew what she wanted. "This one," she said, pointing at a white, broad-winged seagull. "What do you think?"

I took a close look at her: her eyes, her forehead, her imperfect nose.

"Where do you want it?" the tattoo artist asked, preparing his needles.

Noga pointed at the muscle on the small of her back, right above her butt. "Right here," she said.

"You chose the most painful spot," he warned her.

"I know," she said. "I can take it."

The tattoo artist looked at me and asked, "What about you? Don't you want one as well?"

"No," I chuckled, making a face. "This kind of thing isn't for me."

But Noga, already lying on the bed, said, "Wow, that's a great idea. Why don't you get one too?"

I considered this. "I'll think about it," I said.

The tattoo artist placed the catalog in front of me and said, "Go ahead. I'll just finish up with her, it's a small job. It won't take long. Then I'll get to you."

Noga lay on her stomach, shirt off, shorts pulled down. I could see the crack of her buttocks. Why was she getting it there, I wondered, and for who? I paused the stream of images that had started running through my mind. The tattoo artist etched the needle through her skin carefully. The image she'd chosen was almost miniature.

She twisted her face in a pained smile. "So, Abigail, what did you choose?" she taunted.

The artist asked her not to speak because it made her move.

I flipped through the colorful pages—flowers, dragons, animals, magic spells. The tattoo artist invaded her skin, just to the right of the tender area around her spine. I closed my eyes. What animal would I like burned into my skin? Maybe a lioness, though that would be pretentious. Not a bird, I'm not light. Not a gazelle, that wasn't me. Perhaps a mole, a crow, a vampire—creatures who move stealthily through the night. I pictured the two of us naked and tattooed in the prairie, hunched on hands and knees, Noga out on the hunt, lithe, aggressive, while I lingered behind her, heavier but still ready to pounce. Blood droplets emerged on Noga's skin, the room started to spin, and I saw black. A Star of David, a sword, a decapitated head, Venus de Milo, the innocent face of a child. I felt myself sinking, just moments away from passing out.

"Your mother's asleep," I heard the artist tell Noga through my closed eyes. The sun, I thought, or the moon, the dark side of the moon. A gun, or the large cock of a man.

"No, I'm awake," I said, opening my eyes and shaking myself, forcing a smile.

"I'm finished," the guy said. "Come take a look, Mom."

I got up, dizzy, to take a look at the small seagull surrounded by blood, before he covered it with a bandage.

He told Noga to remove the bandage carefully the next evening and not to get it wet until then. "So what about you?" he asked.

I shook my head. "I don't know what I want," I explained. "I need more time to think."

"All right," he said, "these things can take time. No rush. I'll be around."

"Thanks, Mom," Noga said with a smile as she buttoned her shorts. "This is a dream come true." She kissed my cheek.

As we walked out of the studio, I asked, "Would you want me to be your mother?"

She thought about it and said she didn't know.

"You shouldn't," I said. "If I were your mother you'd never be able to soar. I'd run you over with good intentions."

"Let's get a drink," Noga said. "This conversation is too heavy for me right now, and you're looking super pale."

11

FRIDAY NIGHT. Shauli was home, and a few of his military friends who'd come to the big city for a good time came by to pick him up. Tan and skinny like him, they looked around our apartment curiously. They had the fast, broken speech of newbies, thickening their voices to sound manlier.

"Have a seat," I told them. I served them cake, which they politely eviscerated. I asked them where they were from and how basic training was going, careful not to play the role of mental health officer, mindful not to embarrass Shauli. He was quiet around them, restless, hardly speaking. He was still trying to fit in, as if he were being tested. I didn't know if he'd told them he had no father and what kind of explanation he'd given. Then he took them into his room, where they allowed themselves to laugh, to raise their voices, and asked him to play the guitar for them. He strummed the opening chords to "Hotel California."

They rummaged through his drawers. I heard them joking about the things they found in there, until finally Shauli came out and said, "Mom, give me the roof keys. I'll take them upstairs. It's a little too early to go to the party."

Our building was old, built almost eighty years before. It needed a renovation—the plaster was peeling, the walls were cracked and covered with damp spots. But it had an open roof that overlooked the city, not from the immense height of new apartment towers, but from a more human level, and it offered a breeze even on the hottest evenings. Shauli and his friends took the stairs up, hooting and hollering like young men. I couldn't change into a nightgown because I wasn't sure when they'd be back. I looked for something to watch on TV but nothing grabbed me—I was too preoccupied, I wasn't calm. I had the deranged thought of calling Rosolio just to hear the sound of his voice and tell him his soldier son was home on leave, or text him a picture of me in my underwear, home alone on a Friday night. *Want to come over?*

The windows were open. It was a summer evening. I heard them laughing up above, talking out loud, singing silly songs. They're soldiers, I told myself, not theater critics. This is their moment to celebrate their masculinity. And stop worrying about Shauli like it's his first day of kindergarten. He's doing fine. They like him, it's obvious, and they'll learn to appreciate his tenderness. Every military company has one guy with the soul of an artist who plays the guitar.

A knock at the door. The downstairs neighbor. He and his wife were relatively new to the building and I couldn't remember his name.

"I apologize about the time," he said, "but I take it that's your son making a racket up there."

I tried to sound cordial. "They're soldiers on leave, you can understand that. They'll go out in a little bit and you'll have your peace and quiet."

"They're waking up our baby," the neighbor insisted.

"I apologize, but like I already told you, they're soldiers, and they're heading out soon. Why don't you go upstairs and explain the situation to them yourself? They're big boys. What do you want from me?"

"I've tried that already," he said. "They're drunk and won't listen to me. If you ask me, they're smoking weed up there, too. This is an apartment building, not a . . . nightclub." He clearly wanted to say "whorehouse."

"Fine, I'll go up there in a minute," I said. I wasn't about to lose my head over him.

I took the stairs up quietly without turning on the stairwell light. I glanced out through a small window at the doorway to the roof. Six young men on the roof, drinking vodka and arrack and smoking cigarettes. Shauli was drinking but not smoking, he hated cigarettes. Well, what did you expect them to do on a Friday night after weeks on base? I asked myself. Read a Grossman novel? One of them had a portable speaker that was playing whiny love songs, but there wasn't a single girl around them to dilute the atmosphere. I didn't go out onto the roof and didn't say a word to them. Instead, I quietly walked downstairs and out onto the street. I wanted to get some air and knew the neighbor would be knocking at my door again, fuming. If he wanted, he could go up to the roof and deal with them himself. Either he'd convince them to turn it down, or they'd beat the crap out of him. It wasn't my problem.

I sat on the bench on the other side of the street beneath the large poinciana tree, under the cover of darkness. I watched my building and my illuminated apartment, and thought about all the many evenings I'd wasted in there, locked in a box. I recalled Mandy telling me how his team used to observe homes before infiltrating in order to kill somebody inside. Upstairs, Shauli's hoopla could be heard, an island of chaos in the middle of our silent street. A few neighbors walked out onto their balconies, searching for the source of the noise. They might call the police soon.

But around midnight, Shauli and his friends stormed out of the building and went off to their party. They spilled out of the stairwell in a single lump, doubled over with laughter, and by this point Shauli looked just like one of them. Good, I thought. His life depended on them. When they were gone, serenity returned to our street and the neighbors could plummet into their good sleep.

*

Mandy came to town to meet with a gallerist and plan his new exhibition. He would be showing new work for the first time in years, and he was excited. He'd made plans to meet his grandchildren afterward and asked me to join him and try to speak to his daughter, to see if there was any chance of a reconciliation.

The gallerist narrowed her eyes at me. She was a little older than I, with red-framed glasses and fair eyes. She had a nice figure. I pictured Mandy having sex with her, and the thought simultaneously revolted and aroused me. They debated how to present the work without asking my opinion, and then made a guest list. The gallerist said there was a new generation of art collectors, young people with money who weren't familiar with Mandy's work, and this was his opportunity to introduce himself to them.

"Is your father still alive?" she asked me when Mandy went to the bathroom.

I was surprised by this, because until this point she'd practically ignored my existence. "Yes, he's alive," I said.

"He's the analyst, right? My mother was a patient of his," the gallerist said. "Years ago, when I was just a girl, she had a crisis and said your father saved her life. I think she fell in love with him. Her eyes sparkled when she spoke about him."

"That's very possible," I said. "Falling in love is quite common in therapy, and he's a striking man."

"You think anything happened between them?" Her smile was unpleasant.

"I don't think so," I said coolly.

"Well, praise be to the believer. Her name was Yiska. She was a very beautiful woman, much prettier than me. Ask your father about her, I wonder what he'll say," she said, shooting me a cynical look, my least favorite kind. She still wouldn't let go. "Is that how you made Mandy fall in love with you, by using your psychologist superpowers?"

I blushed and said, "Ask him." Mandy and I never said a word about love, and now this intruder was invading our relationship.

"A terrible woman," I told Mandy on the cab ride downtown to see his daughter. He laughed and said I was overreacting. The suspicion she'd raised about my father filled my mind. "I don't like cynical people," I said. Mandy told me not to waste my thoughts about her, she wasn't worth it, but as a gallerist she was very efficient, and she truly loved his art.

Mandy was nervous about meeting his daughter. He briefed me as if we were heading out to a military operation: Her husband wasn't home at the moment; he worked late. When Mandy came over she'd go out and leave him with the children. "My plan," he said softly, as if we had to keep our voices low on the way to meet our target, "is to take the kids out to get pizza or ice cream or whatever they want, and leave you at home with her so you can talk."

"So you've scheduled us a session at home. I never do that," I grumbled.

Mandy said he was willing to sacrifice everything to make peace with his daughter.

"What does 'everything' mean?" I asked skeptically. "Even your art?"

He couldn't answer that.

"All right, Mandy," I said. "I'm happy to do this for you, but don't say things you don't mean. Not to me."

One of the grandchildren opened the door, small and barefoot, and the other ran over to join him. They'd been looking forward to Mandy's arrival. His daughter was standing in the middle of the living room, her face frozen, dressed and ready to go out, a plump young woman with dark, flowing hair. Without looking at him, she announced she'd be back in an hour. The children were young, six-and-a-half and three. They smiled and Mandy spread his arms to hold them close. "I was thinking of taking them out, if you don't mind. We can go to the playground and then to get some ice cream. What do you say?"

The children cheered, "Yes, yes!" The daughter made a face, but the kids jumped up and down, crying, "Ice cream! Ice cream! Mom, say yes!"

Finally, she said, "Go ahead, just bring them back in an hour."

The children put on their sandals, and I asked her quietly if I could stay and talk to her.

"Who are you?" she asked suspiciously.

"I'm a friend of your father, and I'm a psychologist. He asked me to talk to you."

She smiled bitterly. "The man truly has no limits. He brought a psychologist with him. What am I supposed to do with you now?"

I asked her to let me stay.

"Why should I?" she asked. "You're barging into my home and I don't even know you."

The kids ran out the door and down the stairs. "Because I want to help," I said as the door slammed behind Mandy.

"Fine, just for a few minutes," she said. She invited me to sit at the dining table, made me some coffee, and apologized for not having any cookies to offer me. She was trying to quit. I complimented the apartment. She said her husband was the one with the good taste, she only helped. She sat across from me, the insult visible on her pretty, complicated face before she even spoke a single word. "Are you really his friend, or just a professional he hired for this purpose?" she interrogated.

"I'm really his friend," I said. I told her about the therapy sessions I'd had with Mandy, and about my adoration for him as an artist.

"Everybody adores him," she said. "They say he's a real mensch, a strong, quiet man. 'They don't make them like that anymore.' And so talented. That's what people always say. 'You're Mandy's daughter? Lucky you. Oh, what a man.' And I nod like an idiot. Why should I argue with them? Let them think what they want. I know the truth."

I didn't want to shoot straight for the wound. It was too blunt and dangerous. I planned to lead her in a wide arc around him, at a safe distance. But she'd beat me to the punch, taking the reins in her own hands. We weren't in my clinic and I couldn't control the situation. "Do you know about what happened?" she asked. "Did he tell you?"

"Not exactly."

"I quit smoking, that's another small tragedy," she said. "Do you happen to have a cigarette?"

"No, I only smoke one a day, at home in the evening."

"That's some impressive self-control." She smiled, looking pretty as she did so. "I can't handle that."

Their dining area was nice, and I liked Mandy's daughter. She was so much like him.

"What do you want to know?"

"Whatever you'd like to tell me."

She told me about her father, who was the center of their world. They used to orbit around him as if he were the sun. Her mother lived for him, loving him limitlessly, believing he was a genius, that there was no other man like him in the whole world. "I was also totally in love with him," she said. "I remember walking down the boulevard with him. I was very little, I reached up to his knees, and he would talk to me about all sorts of interesting things, all the wonderful places he'd take me when I was older. He pointed out special things on the street, like a singing bird or the twisted roots of a tree. I remember every moment of those walks down the boulevard—who we met, where he bought me some falafel, the weather, every word he said. Mom was a normal thing. She was with me all the time. But Dad was special." She got up, pulled a chocolate bar out of the cupboard, broke off a piece. I took some too, just to be polite. "And then I ask myself why I'm fat," she said.

"You're beautiful," I said.

She glanced nervously at her cell phone. "They'll be back soon," she said. "We don't have enough time. I don't know what we're doing this for."

I told her it was fine, we didn't have to discuss everything right away, I would love to see her again. I felt I'd done my duty and shouldn't step into the darkness with her.

"No," she said, "since you're here, you'd better listen, so you know who you're dealing with. I'll skip ahead. I was a chubby girl. I had body issues as a teenager, but I was still a happy kid. My mother was a lot of help. She gave me strength. I couldn't talk to Dad about these things. He was up on his Olympus, with his art, his exhibitions, his big-deal friends. But fine, I had no complaints, I thought that's what fathers were like. We had our little universe at home, and he had his big universe out there, and the two never mixed, and that was fine. I could grow up in peace."

I now recalled what the gallerist had told me about my father and her gorgeous mother, the thought disrupting my focus like the sound of a steamroller. I couldn't tune it out completely, but I lowered the volume, concentrated on my breathing and on Mandy's daughter's eyes.

She carried on. "In high school I made a new friend, who became my soul mate. We had sleepovers, hung out almost every day. We were like conjoined twins. I'd finally met someone who saw the world the same way as me, someone I could joke around with. And she was a great artist. I envied her. I didn't inherit Dad's gift. What can I say? I'm just an average girl. But I loved her so much that I got over my envy and even talked her into showing her work to Mandy. She was shy at first, but I convinced her that she had to show the world, and that we should start with my father. It was a Friday afternoon. Dad sat on a recliner out on the balcony, drinking arrack and smoking a cigarette while Mom made lunch. 'We want to show Dad something,' I told Mom. She said, 'Of course, of course, go ahead.' She liked my friend, too. I walked over on tiptoes so as not to disturb his artistic thoughts, and told him my friend wanted to show him her art. He looked at her and said, 'Sure, sure you can.' She walked over and pulled a painting out of a folder. Her hands were trembling. He took the painting in his hand, cigarette still in his mouth, and said, 'This is extraordinary. I love it. You're very talented.' He was gushing and she blushed. And that piece of shit—" She slammed her hand against the table, hurting herself.

"We can continue another time," I offered again. This was moving too quickly.

"No, I want you to hear it right now." She raised her voice. I froze. "He invited her to his studio, which was in a small apartment not far from our place. He promised to teach her some techniques without hindering her natural talent. That's what he said, 'We mustn't hinder your natural talent.' At this point, I already realized I'd made a terrible mistake. He was taking her away from me. She'd join the adults, leaving me back with the kids. But I didn't suspect anything beyond that." She glanced at her phone again. I didn't allow phones in my clinic, but I couldn't control that here. "The kids'll be back soon. Once he drops them off, I don't want you two staying here one minute longer." Her eyes were hostile, her body language jumpy. "Anyway, he had a bed in his studio for taking naps on hot summer days and for fucking his whores. And that's where he fucked her, right in front of me. I decided to surprise them one day after school. I knew she was there, and I wanted to be part of their thing. I thought maybe through her he'd start paying more attention to me. So I walked in and saw him on top of her. They were completely naked. The man didn't even shut the door. That's it, you got what you came for. He murdered me that day. You're looking at a corpse."

That took my breath away. I couldn't say a word. I'd planned to offer some explanations, tell her about the trauma Mandy had experienced during military service, that this was his way of dealing with death. I wanted to appease her, but I couldn't. We sat together like mourners. A few minutes later, the kids came home with Mandy, their faces smeared with ice cream, all three of them giddy.

"Let's go," I said when they were still in the doorway, grabbing his hand.

"Just a second, let me say goodbye to the kids," he protested, glancing at his daughter, who was still at the table, her back to him. He hugged the children and they burst inside to holler at their mother about what a good time they'd had, and I pushed him out the door.

"So, how did it go?" Mandy asked.

"I'll tell you later," I said.

We walked silently down the street. He wanted to go out, maybe watch a movie. He'd planned to spend the night at my place, but when we passed the corner I told him I was tired and wanted to be alone.

A bitter disappointment took over his face. "She's poisoned you against me too," he said. "I should have known."

We were standing in the middle of a main street, late-afternoon traffic all around us. "We'll talk later, Mandy," I said. "I'm not fighting with you, I'm not ending anything, I'm too old to do that. This tragedy belongs to the two of you. She told me some things. I need to think. I'll call you, Mandy, I promise."

"When?" he insisted. He was standing on the sidewalk, suddenly looking old, anxious about being left alone.

"Soon, Mandy," I said. "Don't worry, this isn't goodbye." I moved in and fluttered a kiss on his cheek. I wasn't all that brave either.

*

Dad asked me to join him at a philharmonic concert. He'd been a member for ages. After Mom died, Shauli would join him, but now he had no choice but to ask me.

He had trouble walking and didn't want to seem lonely in public. Until we got to the concert hall he leaned against me, lumbering, but as soon as we walked inside he stood up tall, smiled, and walked on without help. He made a royal entrance. I could barely believe my eyes. He had lots of acquaintances there—former patients, people who knew him and Mom socially, university advisees who were now graying men themselves. Dad shook hands and smiled, in no rush to take his seat, while I dawdled behind, knowing almost nobody. I realized this was a show of force: these were his cultured patients and associates, people who listened to classical music, unlike the savages I treated and the brutish military men I'd associated with ever since I was a young woman. I didn't care; I let him show off. I was there to enjoy the music. In recent years I'd learned to love classical music. It spoke to me, and I took pride in that. It meant I was still evolving, things continuing to move inside of me. I read the program. The first piece would be a Mozart concerto. The conductor walked up onstage, followed by the solo violinist. The orchestra began to play as the violinist stood patiently, bow limp, waiting for her moment. Then she raised her bow, arms bare, a young and beautiful woman. She closed her eyes, and as soon as she hit the first note it was as if she were playing inside of me, injecting the music into my nervous system. Everything about her was magical—her movements, her supreme concentration, her smooth, round forehead. At first I worried she might make a mistake, but she soared, no longer on this planet. I looked around to see if others were witnessing this miracle, and I could tell Dad was moved too. I rested my hand on his for a moment, gently, barely touching it. It was a moment of grace. The orchestra joined the violinist on a crescendo. When it was all over she put down her bow, her hair a little mussed, and rested until her next solo. I revealed nothing, but I was upset. I wish Shauli were here, I thought. He's much more sensitive and musically oriented than I am. But he's busy getting strong now, growing rougher and crasser. Isn't that what you wanted when you sent him out there? Just like you let them cut his penis when he was eight days old. Now I couldn't enjoy the music as much anymore. Too many messy thoughts were getting in the way, and the purity of the experience was gone. I tried to get it back but couldn't.

After the concert, in the cab, Dad said this was the kind of evening that made life worthwhile. "What a genius like Mozart is able to say about our existence with just a few notes, normal people like us can't say with a thousand words. And that violinist. . . ." He sighed. The taxi pulled up outside of his building and I supported him up the steps. I felt his skinny frame as he leaned against me. When we reached the door I offered to come in and help him get ready for bed. I suspected it was getting too difficult for him to bathe every day.

"Yes, come in for a moment," Dad said. "But not to help me, I can manage on my own. I want to show you something."

He led me down the hall to his clinic and turned on the light. "Have a seat," he said, pointing to the patient's armchair. I hope he doesn't plan on analyzing me right now, I thought with a start. That would be completely inappropriate. Dad sat down at his desk, his back turned to me, and rummaged through the old wooden drawers.

"What are you looking for, Dad? Can I help you?"

He kept searching the depths of the desk. "There it is," he said, his expression content. He pulled out an old brown envelope. "Sit down for a moment," he said, "I don't like you standing over me like that."

I obediently returned to my seat.

"It's very important to me, Abigail," he began, "to leave this world in a respectable, humane way. Luckily, I've already taken care of that. Years ago, I had a patient, a chemist, who worked in secret laboratories run by the Ministry of Defense. A lonesome, bright man who couldn't find his path. We dove deep. He was a complex, impressive man. Ultimately he left the country and found a job at some big European company. He was grateful to me for helping him reach that decision, so he gave me this envelope as a goodbye gift. Take a look." He signaled for me to come closer, carefully opened the envelope, and revealed a tiny metal shell. "There's a cyanide pill inside," he said.

"What? Why would he give you something like that?" I asked. It was an odd, awkward moment.

"To set me free," Dad said. "So I don't have to depend on others. This is my insurance, my clean and safe passage to death. If I'm in the hospital and can't tell right from left anymore, and my entire existence is nothing but suffering and humiliation, I'm going to need you to help me, Abigail. That's why I'm telling you this. So you know how. Now you know where to find it. You take the pill out and place it under my tongue, that's all. He said it's a special variety that doesn't leave any trace."

I laughed. "It's like something out of an old spy movie. I don't believe one word of it."

"Hand to heart," Dad said gravely, "and you have to promise me. My test results aren't good. The cancer is progressing and the end is near."

No point in arguing, I thought. Why not just make the guy a promise? After all that psychoanalysis and sophisticated outlook on life, things end with a little poisonous pill. "Fine, Dad," I said. "I promise."

"Can I trust you, Abigail?" he asked.

"Yes, Dad," I said, "you can."

"Good girl," he said, "though I don't fully trust you. You're crafty. Maybe I'll ask Shauli as well the next time he visits, just to be on the safe side."

"No, don't bring Shauli into this, Dad, please. Spare him this bit of grisliness."

"I had a dream about him," he said. "A very bad dream."

I didn't want to hear about the dream. The night was getting to be too much for me already. I asked Dad if he needed any help bathing or changing.

"No need," he said with restrained anger, returning the envelope meticulously to the depths of the drawer.

"Good night, Dad, thank you for the beautiful concert," I said, making my way out through the hallway.

12

I SHOWED THE YOUNG BATTALION commanders images of executions from different places around the world—by firing squad, by hanging, by electric chair—one image after the other, in all of which the condemned had their eyes covered. "Why do they cover the condemned man's eyes?" I asked.

"So they don't get scared," a few of them answered.

"No," I said. "That's not it. What do they care if the guy's afraid?" I explained that the condemned man's eyes were covered for the sake of the executioners, so that his gaze didn't cause them to hesitate or drive them mad with remorse.

"How else do we make executioners' jobs easier?" I asked, using my schoolteacher tone. They didn't know, so I told them that one of the shooters in every firing squad received a magazine full of blanks, but they didn't know which one, so each of them was able to enjoy the notion that they weren't the actual killers. I shared my extensive knowledge on the subject and explained the most important rule—that everyone fires at once, as one, so no one can ever tell which shooter delivered the lethal bullet. "They do all this in order to overcome and outsmart the guilt and scruples," I explained.

Their eyes were fixed on the screen. I could have talked for hours about executions in different cultures. I'd always been fascinated by them and had studied them thoroughly.

I turned off the projector and the audience listened in silence. "Human society could not exist without a conscience," I said. "Freud says the conscience first appeared in sons who'd murdered their cruel, omnipotent fathers. That was the beginning of culture. But in war, conscience becomes a burden. It weakens us, so we've got to find ways around it. Do you know who this man is?" I showed them a clip from an interview with an older man in a suit who looked like an old-fashioned businessperson. There was not a single interesting feature in his face, and he spoke calmly and calculatedly. I paused it a few seconds in. "Do you know who this is?" I asked again. Then I showed them the image of smoke mushrooming over Hiroshima. Now it was easier to guess. It was the pilot who'd dropped the atomic bomb. In the interview, conducted in the 1960s, Paul Tibbets said he regretted nothing, that he did what he had to do, and that although he'd killed many, he'd saved the lives of many others. "If Tibbets had to walk down the streets of Hiroshima and individually shoot the tens of thousands of people the bomb had killed, women and men and children, he would have had a much harder time," I told my students. "Technology helps us kill, not only because of the efficiency it offers, but because it makes it mentally much easier and cleaner."

"Say, doctor," the artillery officer who liked to challenge me said, "have the Arabs also heard of this theory of yours about conscience and morality? They don't seem to have any problem killing—from up close, from far away, with a knife, without a knife, whatever. Have you ever studied that?"

I took a deep breath. "I haven't," I said. "But I have no reason to assume things are any different for them. We know the human soul shares certain traits across natural variation."

A rustle of mockery rose from the audience.

"But what about their culture?" the artillery officer asked. "What about their upbringing? Have you ever seen the way they slaughter a lamb on the street during holidays, smearing the blood on their children's faces and their own? Have you forgotten how they lynched our soldiers, then walked out onto the balcony to present their bloody hands for all to see?"

"I haven't looked into that," I admitted. "But I have no reason to think Arab psychology operates differently. I've seen no studies that show that."

"That's because you only run the studies that suit you. If it doesn't fit your agenda, you don't look into it," he said.

"I've got no agenda," I said, "and I don't offer consulting services to the Arabs, I offer them to our military. Don't get me mixed up in affairs I've got nothing to do with." I could feel myself getting defensive. He'd cornered me.

"I don't accept your theory," he said decisively. "I think the Arabs think in a completely different way than us. We're built differently. You can't compare us with them."

"You're entitled to your own opinion," I said. "I'm talking about science here. It's only natural for you to think we're a unique breed of people. It's fine."

But the artillerist wouldn't leave me alone. "By the way, out on the battlefield I don't see any of this hesitation you're mentioning. The guys shoot without any problems. Maybe your studies are relevant for a different time or place, but not to us." He thought he had me beat, that he'd managed to undermine my authority. I could see the ridicule on his face.

"I don't know how many battles you've been in, but you've got your eyes closed," I told him. "Maybe you ought to have a conversation with your friends from the infantry corps sitting right next to you, they'll tell you otherwise. Look up the percentage of shell shock survivors from the most recent operations. You'll discover some ugly realities. Read battle inquiries, see how many soldiers charged ahead and how many got stuck behind. You're speaking out of intuition, while I deal with this stuff as science; that's the difference between the two of us."

And how many battles have you been in? a voice inside me asked as I walked offstage. *How many people have you killed? And how can you speak about these things with such confidence?* None of them mentioned that, of course, but suddenly I felt that I might be faking it, that for some reason I wasn't totally convincing myself. I stood up tall and smiled at the officers as I walked among them on my way out the door.

I felt stifled, as if the air had grown viscous and there was no space between days or actions anymore. Everything was a single sequence without breaks or highlights.

I googled my name every day just to make sure I still existed; I came up with a few results, some professional papers I'd written, a few interviews I'd given years ago about shell shock, when I was still in service and we had come up with a new treatment plan. There were no newer mentions. I'd faded into the ether.

On the other hand, I saw Rosolio wherever I looked. He popped up on news alerts on my phone and in the newspaper at the coffee shop. *The military is prepared for war*, he said, *and this time, we will strive for a decisive victory*. The papers said he was touring the field a lot, visiting soldiers, keeping watch across the border. He was implementing my advice, I noted. But it had been a few months since the Victory Workshop meeting, and I had yet to be summoned to see him again. Perhaps he'd mistakenly thought I'd had enough of military affairs, or perhaps Shauli's enlistment had deterred him. I should show him my eagerness, wag my tail a little. I almost dialed his number many times, then thought better of it, until one day I swore out loud and settled myself. After the line rang a few times, his head of office answered aggressively, "Who's this? Who's calling? How did you get this number?"

I have it because Rosolio fucked me three times during one unforgettable night, I almost said. *I'm the mother of his child. Who are you to tell me off?* Instead, I introduced myself properly—*Abigail, lieutenant colonel, reserve duty, remember me, I've been there a few times for meetings.*

She still sounded surprised. "It's just that this is a private number," she said. "Only close family members use it."

I explained that I'd known the commander a long time, which is why I had this number, then realized I'd made a mistake. These office managers are no morons; she'd draw her own conclusions.

"The Chief of Staff is busy," she said. "I'll let him know you called. But please don't use this number again. You can call the office."

Fine, evil woman, I won't call him again. "Please just let him know that I'm here and happy to help," I told her.

"I certainly will," she said, hanging up.

My helpless feeling soon lifted when I was called in for another task. The head of the Behavioral Sciences Branch, the one who'd taken over my old position, phoned me one morning. "We've got a problem with the snipers on the border," she said. "Too many rioters on the other side are being killed and it's hurting our public relations. They asked us to get involved. Do you feel like going over there, Abigail? Meeting with the soldiers?"

I wasn't surprised that she'd contacted me. My paper, "Psychological Aspects in the Role of the Sniper," based on interviews with dozens of snipers, had made waves at the time throughout the military. Rosolio had called me to say he'd read the article. He praised me and said few people understood the complexity of the soldier's soul as well as I did. Coming from Rosolio, who wasn't generous with praise, this was a formidable compliment. The head of Behavioral Sciences also knew I liked being out in the field with the soldiers. When we got together for a meeting she presented me with the data and we brainstormed appropriate investigation methods. We decided that, as a first step, I'd meet the sniper team with the highest rate of lethal hits (though their score was not much higher than the others') and report my conclusions to her.

I arrived in the evening, having been told the team was busy during the day. We sat at the clubhouse of the base where they were staying, near the border. They were like a wandering troupe, moving from one area of the country to another according to where they were needed. Nineteen snipers were gathered to see me. They all looked like Shauli's friends. I was greeted by their officer, a first lieutenant named Jonah, a skinny guy with long and smooth limbs, like a Modigliani portrait. As soon as I showed up he asked to speak to me privately. He wanted to know if this was an inquiry committee.

"No," I said, explaining diplomatically that I was sent to offer my impressions of the atmosphere in their unit.

"But why did they send a mental health officer? Do they think there's something wrong with us?" His tone was insulted.

"No, of course not," I assured him. "I'm not here as a mental health officer, but as a consultant. You've got nothing to worry about with me. I'm on your side. I'm here to help."

I asked the soldiers to arrange their seats in a semi-circle around me. I was wearing civilian clothing—a casual blouse and pants. I looked like I could be their mother. I told them this meeting was not being recorded, that I wouldn't be quoting anyone by name, and promised that nothing they revealed would be used against them in any legal or disciplinary action. I told them a little bit about myself, including the fact that I had a son in paratrooper basic training, so they realized I was on their side and could lower their defenses.

After easing their minds, though not completely eliminating their suspicious expressions, I asked them to tell me about sniping. There were some awkward giggles until the first soldier volunteered to speak. He gave the official version, saying their mission was to prevent terrorists from crossing the fence, getting into Israel, and killing civilians. "We don't just shoot for no reason," he said, pride in his voice. "We're like surgeons. We only remove the infected limb in order to save the rest of the body. No one who deserves to be hurt gets hurt. We don't shoot innocents."

I nodded. I examined the dynamic between them, their body language, the looks their delicate, slender commander sent them from the side. After they finished repeating these slogans, I asked them to speak more specifically about the work itself. They explained shooting procedures, how to decide who to shoot, who gives the green light.

"How do you feel when you shoot?" I asked once the formal framework was clear to me. "Please, I'd like to hear from someone who hasn't spoken up yet."

One of them, a young man with a pimpled face, whispered a response. I had to ask him to raise his voice. He said it was unpleasant to see a person wounded or dead, but the telescopic viewfinder enabled them to see exactly what happened. "One time, I hit someone in the head," he said. "There was only a small hole in the front of his head, but half his skull blew off in the back."

"How did that make you feel?" I asked.

He said it didn't feel good, but that he had no choice. The guy had been hurling rocks and Molotov cocktails at our soldiers, trying to break through the fence with wire cutters. He had to be taken down.

I asked why he'd shot the man in the head rather than the feet.

The soldier hesitated, then finally said awkwardly, "That's what the commander told me to do. He told me to neutralize him."

First lieutenant Jonah, sitting tall at the end of the line, nodded and said, "In that case we had no choice. I received approval from the battalion commander, who agreed the man had to be taken out."

"When you say it didn't feel good," I asked the teenager, "what exactly do you mean?"

He glanced sheepishly at his friends. They never discussed these things, and now a strange woman had shown up, asking him to open up in front of them. There was a pause, then he said, "I felt like I wanted to throw up. It was just gross. But I got over it by the next time it happened. I don't mind it much anymore. I still feel that way sometimes, but much less. I don't know why it happens. I'm only doing my job, I'm not doing anything wrong."

I didn't ask if they thought about the people they shot, their lives or families, because that could demoralize them. It didn't suit the stage they were at. I could talk about this kind of thing with Mandy, from the distance of years, but not with these youngsters who were going to have to shoot their rifles again the next morning.

"Do you hate them?" I asked.

They looked at each other, searching for the correct answer. They were all very serious, just like their commander, as if they'd been forbidden to smile.

"They're targets and we have to take them out," one of them, with curly hair and big brown eyes, said. "I do hate them. Their faces are evil. They want to kill us for no reason. They're capable of killing children too, you can see it in their faces as they approach the fence."

I quickly took down some notes. "What do you think, commander?" I asked Jonah, who looked tense the entire time.

"I don't have much to add," he said reluctantly. "We never shoot for no reason. As far as I'm concerned, this isn't about my feelings. I don't hate them. We're on a mission. Even though we've got good reasons for hating them."

"There was a woman who was killed, too, and some children," I said, recalling the information the military had presented to me. "Do you feel differently when you shoot a child or a woman?"

This time, Jonah interjected. I could tell they were in awe of him. He said, "We never aim at children. There were a few cases when they were hit by ricochets. The other side lies about the victims' ages. Sometimes they say a seventeen-year-old was thirteen. I'll say it again, you've got to understand, we don't just shoot for no reason. We get a green light for every move we make."

"And what about the young women you've hit?" I asked.

A few heads lowered. No one responded. I'd touched a nerve. Their commander's presence also made it difficult for them to speak openly. Whenever I asked about how they felt he fidgeted or made a face. He didn't want me spoiling the hermetic system he'd designed for them. He was right, of course—that was the only way to survive their role. But I knew very well that after they got discharged, grew older, and were no longer surrounded by friends, the images would begin to strike mercilessly.

"We very rarely shoot at women," Jonah answered for them, "and when we do, it's never with an aim to kill. There have been a few cases when stray bullets accidentally hit women. It happens. It isn't our fault. I don't know why they even let girls come to the fence. They want us to kill them so that we look evil."

I let them go. They left the room quietly. There was none of the cheerful camaraderie one usually witnesses among fellow soldiers. I told Jonah I wanted to go see their work on the field, and that I would coordinate with headquarters.

"Sure, you should come," he said, to my surprise. "When you're with us, the world will seem different." Then he smiled at me for the first time.

Once, years ago, I met Arik Sharon. This was while the military prepared for the Gaza Pullout—the dismantling of Israeli settlements in the Gaza Strip. I advised the High Command on how to construct messaging that would convince soldiers that their mission was just. We were facing a challenge: typically, the military served and protected the people, but here they were supposed to evict their own from their homes. So the General Staff requested our assistance in implementing the appropriate emotions, preparing soldiers for the moment when they had to drag men, women, and children out of their houses. So they didn't lose their nerve, so they were able to endure the curse words, the rotten eggs, and the bags of feces that would be hurled at them without being derailed toward violence. The military had prepared a detailed model for the day of evacuation, in which all scenarios were rehearsed. Arik Sharon came by to watch the preparation process and give the soldiers a boost. Then he participated in a High Command staff meeting. When it was over, we were introduced. I was a lieutenant colonel in uniform at the time and stood at attention before him, touched by the situation. He was smaller than I'd imagined, his face more delicate than it appeared in photographs. He said he was impressed with the contribution I'd made during the meeting, then added with a little smile, "In my time, we didn't need psychologists. We just performed the task. I don't think Ben-Gurion ever consulted a therapist." Everyone around him laughed. The Chief of Staff laughed, the head of the High Command laughed, and the senior officers laughed. I was the lowest-ranking officer there.

"On the contrary, maybe if Ben-Gurion had consulted with a good psychologist, on the morning of the Altalena Affair," I said, voice shaking with emotion, "he might have avoided the battle altogether and spared the nation some trauma."

An awkward silence fell, until finally Arik chortled, that famous muscle tic acting up near his nose. "Good point," he said, "you very well might be right. Thank you." Then he left. He was a gentleman. Once again, I was the gifted student, the slightly mischievous know-it-all whom the teachers were fond of, even when she was a little out of line. I imagine Arik forgot all about me moments after he walked away.

13

A MESSENGER DELIVERED a package that was addressed simply, *To Abigail*. The unique handwriting told me it was from Mandy. Perhaps he'd mailed me his dick, having chopped it off with a sculptor's scalpel and placed it carefully in a box to atone for his sins. I was relieved when I opened it and found a whittled, dark brown wooden figurine of a naked, bowing man with a long back and an invisible face in a pose of contrition. I was deeply touched. I called him. "You should send it to your daughter, not me," I said.

He said he'd made two and sent her one as well. "She did something stupid after you met her," said Mandy. "It isn't your fault, of course, but she took some pills and spent half a day in the hospital. She's fine now. Her husband spoke to me. She asked that I not come see the kids for a while."

I felt a piercing pain in my heart. "Oh my God, of course it's my fault," I said. "I shouldn't have intervened. I approached her crudely and unprofessionally. I wish I'd never gotten involved in this at all."

"No, that isn't true," said Mandy, his voice deep and warm like the wood of the figurine. "It isn't your fault."

The wooden man stood on the table in front of me, bowing. I had trouble breathing. "You think she'd want to see me?" I asked, hoping I could still repair something.

"No, Abigail," he said, "leave her alone. This wound can't be healed."

I nodded in the empty room. I missed his hand and his wise eyes. "The sculpture is beautiful." I picked it up and felt it. "I'm sorry about your daughter. I hope she'll at least let you keep seeing your grandchildren."

"When are you coming to visit?"

"Not right now, but I will. I'm feeling cramped down here," I said.

I wondered what his daughter had done with her matching figurine, whether she'd tossed it in the trash or hurled it furiously against the floor, shattering it.

The next day, after my conscience tormented me all night, I defied him and went to see her. I wanted to make sure she was all right. It was midmorning on a weekday, when her kids were at school and she was home alone. When she came to the door I could detect no exterior signs of distress beyond paleness and black circles under her eyes. She hadn't cut her wrists or hanged herself, she'd only taken pills. She looked at me, debating. "Please, come in," she finally said.

We sat in the living room this time, on a soft couch stained with food and finger paint.

"I was sorry to hear about what happened," I said.

She answered, "It's over. A silly mistake. I'm fine now."

I took a deep breath. I was relieved. She was alive. I hadn't killed her. So why had I come back? All I could do here was cause her more pain. I got up and said, "I'm glad to see you're all right. I'll go now. I was just in the neighborhood and wanted to say hello."

"Hang on," she said, "stay a bit. I read up on you a little. I saw you're an expert in treating shell shock survivors. Do you think that's what's wrong with him?"

"I do."

She considered this, then said, "So your theory, if I understand correctly, is that because Dad served in the Commando and killed Arabs with his own hands, and watched his friends die, he then had to fuck seventeen-year-old girls, and especially his daughter's best friend, correct?"

"That's not what I'm—"

"Answer the question." We were sitting close together on the couch. I could smell her breath. There was none of the distance I maintained in the clinic. "I found an interview with you online. I think I get your way of thinking now. Eros and Thanatos, that whole deal. Don't look so surprised, I'm not an idiot, I understand a thing or two. In the interview you said men kill and are killed, that's what they were born to do, and that between one killing and the next they have to unload their sexual urges, otherwise they can't function."

"Not exactly," I said, "that's simplifying a little, but the general idea is right. I didn't come up with that theory, greater people did. Men are motivated by their urges, like forces of nature."

"That's so disappointing," she said, turning away from me.

"Of course, that doesn't justify—"

"That's the excuse you give them," she said, raising her voice. "You're a collaborator. As far as I'm concerned, have them stop killing if that's the price of their wars. They should just stop. I never asked them to kill in my name."

"But we can't just stop," I said softly.

She raised her voice higher, almost yelling. "Can you hear yourself? Whose side are you on? Life or death? Ours or theirs?"

I lowered my head. I was sorry I'd come empty-handed instead of bringing flowers, or maybe something for the children—some candy or a toy.

She wouldn't let go. "What is our role, as women?" she insisted. "To serve as comfort blankies and a place for them to park their dicks? How do we fit in in this awful world of yours?"

"That's up to us," I murmured, picturing Noga's strong, wise face. "We can kill too."

"That's your solution? For us to kill? This is unbelievable."

I got up to leave again, this time for good. "Your father misses his grandchildren. At least let him see them."

"It's too hard right now," she said. "He'll just have to wait."

"Is anyone helping you? Are you in therapy?" I asked.

"My husband helps," she said. "The kids give me strength. I'm on medication. I just need to survive one day at a time. I keep trying for the kids' sake. If it weren't for them, I would have given up long ago."

When I left, instead of thinking ill of Mandy, I thought kindly of him. I missed him. I felt sorrier for him than I did for her. I forgave him.

*

Friday afternoon. Shauli was playing the guitar behind the closed door of his bedroom. How I'd missed that. His dirty laundry was tossing and turning in the machine after three weeks away, and I was prepping a chicken for dinner, fulfilling my maternal duty. The noise around us had died down for a moment. I was barefoot, a young mother on her own again, crushing tomatoes and mixing in some olive oil to enrich his diet and get him used to solids, then slowly spoon-feeding him. For a few months when he was a baby, we lived in our own perfect little world: home, out to the park, nursing, nap time, loving gazes, reading him stories before he understood a single word of them, an early-evening bath in lukewarm water and baby soap, clean diaper, smile, tickling little feet. It went on like this for three months before I went back to work, thinking the military couldn't go on without me.

Shauli came out of his room in a T-shirt and shorts, having locked his rifle in the closet. I searched for his eyes, hoping he'd sit down for a moment and tell me how he was doing. "You played beautifully," I told him.

He said his high school band was going to perform the following night at a fresh-voices showcase, and that they'd asked him to play even though he'd missed most of the rehearsals. "Sure, do it, sounds like fun," I said. "Can I come?"

"Why not? Come along."

"Why don't you invite your friends from the military too?" I suggested.

Embarrassed, Shauli said, "No, that doesn't feel right."

I fell silent, tensed up, searching for something to say that wouldn't spoil his mood. I just wanted him to feel good on his leave. Communication with our children is simple when they're little and need us, but later on it becomes so complicated.

He looked up at me, finally letting me meet his eyes, which were red with fatigue and sun, and said, "It's going to be my last show. I think I'm quitting music."

"Why?" I cried.

"I've lost the taste for it. I'll never be Jimi Hendrix, I know that much. Tomorrow's the last time."

"Don't be hasty," I said. "You've got your whole life ahead of you, and I think you're a great musician."

"It just doesn't fit," Shauli said sadly, his voice trembling a little. I was the only one who'd be able to notice it.

"Why not? You'll be discharged eventually and you'll want to get back to it."

"It'll be too late."

"Do you want to drop out of the paratroopers, Shauli?" I asked.

He widened his eyes, his expression distant and foreign, and said, "No, I can't drop out now."

Then he took his surfboard to the beach. I watched him from the balcony until he disappeared around the corner, free for a moment, wearing a colorful swimsuit in the flickering shadow and light.

In the late afternoon, he took the car and picked up Dad, who could no longer walk the short distance from his apartment to mine. Sitting at the dinner table, I told Shauli about the concert and the fantastic violinist who'd played Mozart. Dad said little, his eyes constantly on Shauli. We resisted the urge to argue, knowing that every word we said could act like gunpowder.

"Is it harder now?" Dad asked in the middle of dinner, and Shauli gave a noncommittal response. We both noticed the mental blocks that he'd built up since his enlistment. I hoped it was just exhaustion.

"I'm worried about him," Dad whispered to me after dinner, when Shauli stepped away from the table to talk on the phone. "He's closing up." Dad's face was the gaunt essence of worry.

"He's tired and needs company," I said softly.

His eyes sharp, Dad said, "I don't think that's it at all. It's much more fundamental with that."

We both fell silent as Shauli returned to the table.

YISHAI SARID

We tried to be responsible this time, putting off our little council meeting for another time, when he wasn't around.

I came to the Saturday night show on my own. It took place at a club in a neighborhood filled with garages and workshops, a large space on the second floor of a building, lots of noise, very crowded. I was old enough to be everyone's mother, but I looked all right in jeans and a T-shirt, and if anyone thought I was too old to be there, that was their problem. I passed the time until Shauli's band went up by listening to the other performances. I bought a beer and found a concrete pillar to lean against. I adjusted to the rhythm, and the horrendous volume was good for blocking out my thoughts. A guy with a thick beard who looked to be around thirty came up to me and said, "Are you here on your own?"

I confessed that I was. I found it amusing.

"Do you mind if I stand next to you?"

"No, of course not."

"Can I buy you another beer?"

"Why not? Go ahead. My son's about to perform."

"Great," the guy said, seeming excited by this notion.

"There they are!" I cheered. My head was already spinning a little from the alcohol. Shauli's band went up

186

onstage dressed in vintage London style, Shauli wearing the black leather pants I'd bought him when we'd gone there together.

"Which one's your son?" the guy asked.

"The one with the buzz cut."

"He's a soldier?"

I nodded. "Yeah, a soldier."

They had some issues at first, some feedback, but they started over, and in a matter of seconds everything worked out. They got into the groove, their singer swallowing the mic, Shauli standing gorgeously next to him, a little to the back, his guitar against his thighs, every strum caressing me with pain.

The bearded guy put his arm around me.

"Don't," I said, moving away from him. I pushed my way closer to the stage, wanting to hear them up close. They'd all been to my home with their pimply faces, eating my food, locking themselves in Shauli's bedroom, thinking I had no idea what they did there, and now they were kicking ass onstage, making the room spin with their noise, closing their eyes with pleasure. Put rifles in their hands instead of those guitars, I thought, and give an order to remove the safety. It's the same kind of energy motivating them. They played three songs, then an encore by demand of the infatuated audience. I didn't go up to Shauli afterward, I didn't want to cramp his style. That's all he needed, to walk offstage like a rock star and then have his mother glom onto him.

"Are you leaving?" the bearded guy asked, popping up beside me again. "Can I walk you?"

I smiled and said my husband was waiting for me at home.

If I were Shauli, I thought on the way to the car, I wouldn't go back to base tomorrow morning. I'd find a way to escape—by boat, by foot. I wouldn't let them trap me.

I don't know when he came home that night, but when I woke up the next morning at 5:30 to drive him to the train station he walked out of his room wearing his uniform, heavy pack on his back, rifle strap across his chest, rubber bands securing the ends of his pants, clean-shaven and very put together, as if the man I'd seen onstage the night before had been somebody else. I made him some coffee and cut a piece of cake. He ate and drank with haste.

"Last night was great," I said on the way to the station. "What did you do afterward?"

Yawning, Shauli said he'd come home and gone to sleep.

"Hold on, Shauli," I said as he got out of the car and loaded the pack onto his back. "You'll give me a call if things get too hard, right?"

He mumbled a "yes" and disappeared into the throng of morning commuters.

*

Mandy called and asked to meet me in my clinic, for a fee, he emphasized, just like in the beginning.

"Fine," I said, "but I won't charge you. Don't be silly."

I was embarrassed by my appearance. The lesions on my fingers had spread onto my nails. I considered wearing a pair of silk gloves I'd found in my mother's closet after she died, because Band-Aids no longer did the trick. Finally, I decided I'd face him as I was.

"There's one thing I haven't told you," he said right off the bat. "I feel like I've fooled you, and maybe that's what dropped the wedge between us. It has to do with what happened with my daughter. That's why I wanted to meet here, so you can know the whole truth."

"Go ahead," I said, "I'm listening."

"Everything I told you during our first sessions about what haunts me—it's all true. I don't need to repeat it right now." Mandy's voice turned hoarse and he took a sip of water. "What I didn't tell you, and that's the reason I'm here today, is about the pleasure I felt when I killed someone, the fantastic elation I experienced. Nothing else in life compares to it. I felt so good after the first time that I went to see my commanders and asked to always be the executioner, the one who, after the whole complicated plan was carried out, slit the target's throat or shot them from point-blank range. And they let me have it. I did it well and they could tell I enjoyed it. I crossed every line. I had total power and a sense of freedom you can't even imagine. Not just in the moment, but long afterward. I'm sure some murderers serving a life sentence stay sane only by recreating the memory of the moment they committed their crime, fantasizing about it over and over again. Even now, with all the nightmares and self-loathing, those moments remain the highlights of my life. The hand remembers. The fingers remember. The brain remembers the chills of pleasure."

I listened, feeling a peculiar sense of envy.

"I've cheated you, Abigail," he said. "The things I did afterward weren't an escape. On the contrary, I was trying to return to that pleasure. I couldn't legally kill anyone, so I sought out alternatives. That's where art came from. And fucking. And obscenity. Everything good and bad I ever did."

He looked scarred and ancient like one of his sculptures. I already knew everything he was telling me. The murderousness hidden within them is what draws me to these monsters. I fought the urge to come closer to him, to close the distance between us. My clinic was the last place on earth where order still prevailed, and I must never breach the rules of conduct.

"I know, Mandy," I said after a long pause. "But it's good you told me, anyway."

14

"YOUR FRIEND IS HERE," the bartender, the owner's daughter, said with a smile.

Noga walked in from the lit street to the dimness inside. We hugged for a moment, kissing each other on the cheeks like old friends.

"Are they new?" I asked, looking at her clean, feminine, flat sandals, one thin red strap stretching across the base of her toes.

"Yes, how did you even notice?" She smiled. She was wearing shorts and a collared blouse.

"I love your outfit," I said.

"Thanks, Abigail." Noga looked stronger and more feminine. The weight of responsibility suited her.

I ordered a gin and tonic. "I'll have the same," Noga told the bartender, who smiled at her.

"You're difficult to get a hold of," I said with a smile.

She apologized and said she'd had a few extremely busy weeks at the squadron. She'd been tasked with training the land teams, then she was on call, and last weekend she'd gone camping in the desert with some friends. That all sounds fine, I thought, but why did she want to meet me? She must have a reason.

The elderly owner watched us from the other end of the bar, his eyes falling kindly on both of us with the sage look of one who's seen and heard everything in his time.

"I flew a lot," she said softly, though no one but me could hear her anyway, the music was so loud. "Even above enemy territory, and I was completely fine. I felt good."

"Great."

"Just one thing got in the way," she said, seeking out my eyes. "During my most recent mission I fired at a car loaded with weapons. I hit it perfectly. Nothing was left of it and everyone talked me up when I got back to base, even the squadron commander."

"Fantastic," I said.

"Wait, listen," she said. "A few hours later our intel officer came to talk to me. He's this annoying dude who asked me out once and I turned him down. He asked if I knew who I'd hit in that car. I told him I didn't. I knew I'd eliminated the target, so what did I care exactly who was in there?

YISHAI SARID

"The intelligence officer said, 'You didn't just hit a target, you killed one of their higher-ups.' So I said, 'Great, glad to hear it.' Then he goes, 'And his son.' Okay, I thought. I thought the son must be a terrorist too. 'A child,' he said, 'seven years old, I think.' I pretended like I didn't care, but I felt like he was strangling me. I had trouble speaking after that. I didn't let it show. I didn't talk to anyone about it. I kept flying, but it's been on my mind ever since. I wake up thinking about it and go to bed thinking about it every day." Noga took a big gulp and waited for me to fix her head or at least offer forgiveness, as if I were authorized to do that.

"What's bothering you really?" I asked.

She looked at me quizzically. "What do you mean? I killed a child."

"And if the ugly intelligence officer hadn't told you about it, you wouldn't have known, would you?"

"No, I wouldn't." She gave me a small smile.

"And you didn't know there was a child in the car when you hit it, did you?"

"Of course not," she said. "If I had, I probably wouldn't have bombed it."

"So what are you accusing yourself of really? Accomplishing your mission properly?"

194

Her pretty feet swung underneath her in the new sandals.

"Listen, Noga," I said. She looked sad, and that made me upset. "You didn't know there was a child there. You did the right thing. You probably saved civilian lives. It isn't your fault that they don't keep their children safe, involving them in wars. You're absolutely not guilty of anything here." We should have met in my clinic, not here, I told myself. This isn't professional.

"So what am I supposed to do?" she asked. "Just live with it?"

"Exactly," I said. "You aren't the first or last person who's been in this position, and being a woman is no excuse to dwell on it. Deal with it. Promise me you'll have a ball this weekend and not let that terrorist spoil your leave."

"It's hard," she said. There was a disconnect between her grave expression and her cute summer outfit.

"Nobody cares but you. The boy is dead now, and he didn't feel a thing. Get over it, Noga. This kind of thinking makes you dysfunctional. It's over. Move on. Let's talk about nice things."

"I'm afraid they'll take revenge against me," she said. Now we were getting to the heart of it, the part she hadn't been able to shake off. We were back at the captivity training trauma, and it was my responsibility to fix it again.

"How would they ever reach you?" I asked. "They don't even know who you are."

"They could intercept me, and then I'd be at their mercy," she said, lowering her voice. "The intelligence officer said they already have anti-chopper missiles and they're just waiting for the next war to use them."

"It sounds like the one trying to intercept you is this intelligence officer," I said. "They aren't going to intercept you, Noga. I'm sure you've got ways of preventing that."

"That's what scares me the most, Abigail." She was practically clinging to me, seeking shelter in my body. "And I'm afraid I'll make mistakes out of fear. I can feel it when I fly."

I considered suggesting she come back to therapy, but I knew I had no magic cure to offer and I didn't want to lose our friendship. "Can you put your fear on hold until I figure out a solution?" I asked. I already had the seed of an idea.

"If you promise to find one, then yes," she said, stretching out of her huddled, childish pose. "I already feel a little better. Thank you for helping me."

"That's because I love you," I said. The entire time, the owner's mute gaze hovered over us from the other end of the bar.

*

Nivi's mother informed me that he wouldn't be coming to therapy that week. I asked what had happened, and she said he'd assaulted someone at the grocery store and was involuntarily committed to a psychiatric ward.

"Oh no," I said. I asked her to tell me more.

She said there had been an argument at check-out. Nivi had claimed that the cashier had entered an incorrect price for one of the items and refused to pay until she corrected her mistake. It was a can of imported Greek kalamatas (Nivi's mother said he was especially fond of them). Nivi thought it was on sale and the cashier insisted he'd misunderstood. She called the branch manager and while they waited for her to arrive, someone in line asked that Nivi move along because he was holding up everything. Everyone started raising their voices. Nivi had a bad reaction to the guy and they started fighting. Nivi butted his head into the man, breaking his nose. A commotion ensued and someone called the police. Nivi was arrested. His mother rushed to the station to talk to the cops and explain the situation—that Nivi was mentally ill due to military trauma and needed treatment, so the police contacted the district psychiatrist, who decided to hospitalize Nivi.

"Forgive me," said Nivi's mother, who was very polite, "but Nivi wanted to know if you could visit him at the hospital."

"Of course," I said. I felt a responsibility toward him, and his mother's devotion was moving.

I came to see him the next day. He was in a semi-closed ward, meaning he couldn't leave freely but was permitted visitors. I could tell right away that he'd deteriorated. His movements were especially jumpy and his face kept twisting. I wasn't sure I'd be able to have a conversation with him in his current state.

"You see, Nivi," his mother said, "you wanted Abigail to come, and here she is."

We were sitting in an enclosed courtyard around a wooden picnic table. In the corner was a male nurse in white, keeping watch.

Nivi wore an aggressive smile. "Let me ask you something," he began feverishly, his hands snaking around themselves with constant motion. "You remember I came to see you the day before the operation and told you I didn't want to go, that I was afraid? Remember that?"

This is no good, I thought. "Yes, I remember," I said. I couldn't lie.

Nivi let out a triumphant snort. "I told you," he said, turning to his mother, "and you didn't believe me. You told me you trusted her, that she was the only one who could cure me, not like the others who just choked me with meds. And I wanted to believe it, too. I didn't want to bring up unpleasant memories. But look, Mom, I'm in the hospital again. She hasn't helped me at all."

Now his mother narrowed her eyes at me too.

"Why didn't you listen to me back then?" Nivi demanded. His legs never stopped bouncing.

"I *did* listen to you," I said softly. "You said you were frightened. Fear is a natural sensation for a soldier. We can't leave every frightened soldier behind."

"But I was practically shaking, you've got to remember that. I couldn't even talk right. I told you I was falling apart." Nivi stood up. Other patients in the yard started gathering around us, sniffing out the action. "I begged you not to send me out, and you didn't do anything about it."

"You were an experienced soldier, Nivi, almost all the way to honorable discharge. You'd had a successful service." I tried to keep my cool. "I trusted you to hold on. I had no idea what was going to happen." I didn't tell him that right after he'd left my office I'd called his company commander, who'd said Nivi was just nervous, and that under no conditions should I excuse him from participating in the operation, because it would hurt the other soldiers' morale.

"Why didn't you listen to me?" Nivi bowed and rose repeatedly, like a worshipper. "I told you I couldn't do it, and you ruined my life." All around I heard mumbles of agreement from the other patients. I glanced at the nurse, who was standing too far away. If Nivi attacked me I'd stand no chance. He was much bigger and stronger than me. I didn't like psychiatric hospitals. They were the final stop, the waste disposal site, and I wanted to succeed with my patients. I shouldn't have accepted Nivi for therapy; that had been a mistake.

"This is the first I'm hearing about it," his mother said, "and I don't understand why you haven't told me about this. I don't understand what this means. I'm confused. I thought you were a good therapist, a decent one. . . ."

I had nothing to apologize for. I told his mother, "He was a healthy twenty-year-old soldier who'd undergone challenging paratrooper training without any problem. Fear is not a mental disorder. Everyone's afraid. War isn't normal. He could have been killed. Would you have complained to me then?"

"It isn't right, what you're saying," his mother fumed. "Not everyone is built for war, and those who are weak ought to be taken into account. Look at what happened to him. At least admit you've made a mistake. I don't understand how I ever thought you could cure him."

"Listen to me, Nivi." I tried to catch his raging eyes. In a flash of memory, I looked at the large man standing before me, his body atrophied with medication and disuse, and saw the young soldier who'd come to see me, panicked. Distress gripped my chest. He knew himself and knew he was on his way to oblivion. He'd warned me and begged for help, and I'd done nothing.

"Listen, Nivi," I murmured, "no good will come out of you blaming me for what happened to you. It isn't my fault, it's war's fault, and I'm not in charge of war. I still want to help you. When you get out of here, come see me and we'll continue therapy. I'll do my best to help you."

"I remember your office on base," Nivi said, as if he hadn't heard a word I'd said. "It was nice, not like the other military offices. There was a soft chair and you invited me to take a seat. For a second, I felt like a human being, not military property. And you spoke kindly to me, you smelled good. I felt like you were my older sister. I looked up to you. I remember that day you came to see us on the field, how cool you were. You said you'd discuss my case with the commanders and make sure they'd keep an eye on me, that you understood how hard it was for me. You promised me, but then you didn't do anything about it. Nothing. You killed me." He slapped his thigh, hard, then broke into tears.

A hand touched my shoulder. I jumped. It was the nurse, who murmured that I'd better leave, this was getting dangerous, my presence was causing a commotion.

I wanted to say goodbye to Nivi's mother, but she turned away from me. I walked out quickly, almost running, but my legs were heavy. It felt as if crooked iron pegs were anchoring me to the ground.

I dreamed that the General Staff had posted my obituary in the newspaper, signed by Rosolio. My name and rank appeared inside the small black frame. In my sleep, it seemed to have something to do with a conspiracy we were in on together, some secret mission. I knew I hadn't truly died, but I couldn't be sure, and all night long I tried and failed to recall the details of our heroic plan. I was concerned about how the obituary had made this lie public. People really thought I'd died and I was forbidden from correcting them. I was buried alive, my patients stopped coming in, Shauli mourned me, and I said nothing. Even when I woke up and sat up in bed and made sure I was alive, the pit in my stomach wouldn't go away, and my fingers burned with the tension.

15

I WENT TO VISIT the snipers at their post at the border. It had taken a few weeks before I'd received my permit. I had to convince the head of Behavioral Sciences, who'd sent me on this mission, that the visit was essential for completing my report. I put on the uniform I kept folded neatly in my closet, laced up my black military shoes, and checked myself in the mirror. I didn't look twenty years old, but I didn't look ridiculous either. I looked just fine. I didn't wear my insignia so as not to intimidate the soldiers. I wanted to get an impression of them at their busiest, so I came on Friday morning, when many rioters attempted to cross the border fence. On base, I signed out a helmet, a bulletproof vest, and binoculars. Jonah was conducting roll call, and then we were driven a short distance through a protected road to the rear of the post. Jonah and the soldiers lay down on the ground in pairs, thirty feet apart, each pair consisting of a sniper and a tracker who helped him pinpoint targets and aim his rifle.

Jonah signaled for me to lie down beside him. His rifle was gorgeous. From the research I'd conducted about snipers years earlier, I knew these were extremely expensive rifles, real works of art, handmade in the United States and installed with a telescopic sight. The bullets were stored in an internal magazine called an ovary, not in an exterior one like regular rifles. As we lay at the post, I asked Jonah what was the farthest distance from which he'd ever hit a person, and he said that once he'd killed someone from over half a mile away. My mouth fell open and he laughed and promised me it was true. My marvel and his laughter broke the ice between us. The range was much shorter here. We were six hundred and fifty feet away from the fence. For snipers, that was child's play. Out in the field, Jonah's soldiers looked refreshed and collected, different than the way they'd appeared that night at the clubhouse, and Jonah's beauty glowed among them. His eyes were slightly slanted and his face was so smooth that it looked as if he were wearing makeup. "Are you comfortable?" he asked as we settled on our stomachs on the dirt battery. I said I was. People were already gathering on the other side of the fence, but they were still far away, and Jonah explained that we didn't bother them from that range, only when they got closer. We lay in wait like fishermen waiting for their float to bob. Jonah was communicating over the radio with the battalion commander, who was sitting in a watchtower not far away. For a long while nothing happened and I thought I'd wasted my time coming here. Then some movement began in the distance.

"There," Jonah said, "they're coming closer. Look, they're carrying stuff in their hands and their pockets. This is just an appetizer. They're testing the waters."

A few guys in jeans and sneakers approached the fence, and just behind them walked a young woman in a long-sleeved shirt and a headscarf. I could see through my binoculars that her eyes were painted with kohl. Even here, she wanted the boys to like her. There was a fence between us and them, and behind it a no-man's-land of barren dirt. They shouted slogans. I asked Jonah if he understood what they were saying, and he answered tensely that he didn't speak Arabic. Then, *bam!* One of them threw something toward us—an iron bar, maybe, which landed far away from us—then retreated quickly.

"You see him?" Jonah quietly asked his tracker. The tracker said he did. "I could take him out right now," he explained to me, "but I'm waiting. He hasn't earned his shot yet. Please write in your report that we aren't bloodthirsty."

In the meantime, the gathering on the other side grew rowdier, participants yelling words that scattered on the wind. Jonah, lying next to me, smelled fresh from his morning shower. They held up posters and played music, only the beat of which reached us, without melody. Black smoke rose from the tires they'd set on fire. "That way they can get closer without us spotting them," Jonah explained. "Their goal is to cut a hole in the fence and break in."

The heavy smoke made it harder to breathe. Jonah rested his cheek against the butt of his rifle and concentrated. Inhale, exhale, focus. Just like in meditation, those were essential skills for a sniper. "Here we go," he muttered. On the other side, dozens began storming the fence through the smoke. Jonah whispered on the radio with the battalion commander, marking targets. "Fire," Jonah commanded in a whisper. A second later, a few of the rioters dropped onto the dry dirt, injured, and the clumsy attack was interrupted by cries of rage. I asked if they were dead, and Jonah said that the directive was only to injure them, to hit their legs, but that aiming accurately at a running target wasn't always possible. Through the binoculars, I saw the injured rioters being evacuated. Some were stood up and supported under their arms as they limped away, crying in pain. Others were laid out on stretchers and carried away.

"I don't think anyone's been killed," Jonah said, "but their soccer days are behind them."

The cramped human bundle before us regrouped, and suddenly a few dozens more broke out in a run toward the fence, hurling explosive devices and Molotov cocktails that blew up far away from us. I was impressed by their courage and stupidity. They must have been drugged or utterly brainwashed to volunteer to drop like flies. But they weren't the subject of my examination, they were somebody else's problem.

Whispered coordination began over the radio again. Jonah said, "See the guy in the middle? The one pointing his finger right now? He's the instigator. He's sending them to die."

The tracker pointed him out. A guy in black, like the villain in a karate movie, was urging the boys on with shouts and hand gestures, signaling to them to move toward the fence and try to breach it, sending them to their deaths while he stayed behind.

"Give me your hand," Jonah whispered. No one else could hear him. "Scooch closer." He took my hand gently, spread my fingers, and placed my forefinger on the trigger. "Find him in your binoculars," he whispered. "And now we shoot." Without asking for permission, his finger mounted mine and squeezed. The bullet flew through the long barrel and out on its journey, and within a fraction of a second I saw the man in black grabbing his gut, doubling over, and falling to the ground, a puddle of blood spreading around him. I removed the binoculars. Silence fell all around me. Nothing could penetrate it. I said nothing. I knew any word I would utter would spoil the moment. Jonah shot a few more times in order to block the attack once and for all. I watched his quiet work from the side, and when he put down the rifle for a moment I told him I wanted to leave, that I'd seen enough.

"Fine," Jonah said. He called over a soldier to take me back safely.

"Thank you," I said as I hunched out of the post.

He turned toward me for a moment and looked into my eyes.

When I was back on safe ground I stood up tall, stretched my limbs, and smiled to myself. I felt whole.

Mandy came to town for the opening of his exhibition and noticed the change in me right away. "What's gotten into you?" he asked, searching my face with an artist's eye and a curious smile, trying to guess. I didn't tell him. I've joined you, I thought, in that other world. Now I know what you were talking about. I came with him to his exhibition opening. It was attended by a few dozen people, acquaintances of his and the gallery owner's. We were offered wine, fruit, and less than the finest cheese in disposable dishes. Everyone there was too old, the air was stifling, and I yearned for youth. Mandy stood around drinking cheap cognac, surrounded by some old friends. He entertained them and they laughed at his every word. The older women watched him with adoration. It was a faded image of the court he'd held twenty-five years before, when he was the most charismatic and desirable artist in town and could do with them as he pleased. Even now, standing among them, the compassion was gone from his face, leaving behind nothing but exposed lust. I suddenly realized what his daughter saw in him, what she remembered, and why she hated him and refused to forgive.

"Did you ask your father about my mother?" the gallerist asked, emaciated and evil.

"No," I said, "I didn't get a chance to."

She looked at me incredulously. I didn't like the way she'd exhibited Mandy's work and staged this opening, or even the people she'd invited.

"I'm heading out," I told Mandy softly. "I've got a very busy day tomorrow."

He tried to keep me there longer, but his old acquaintances dragged him back into their circle.

"You should get back to the village," I whispered in his ear before leaving. "Don't stay here too long, these people aren't good for you."

I walked down on the beach, all the way to the dark line of the water, then strolled alongside it for a long time. I had to escape the lights and soothe the thick, dark streams twisting through my mind.

Late that night, Mandy called me, sounding drunk, and asked if he could spend the night. I hesitated. "No, Mandy," I finally said, "I'm sorry, not tonight." I didn't want to sink into his abyss with him. "Do you have someplace else to go?" I asked.

He said, "I've got lots of options, all I need to do is choose among my elderly fans, but I'm afraid they'll assault me in the middle of the night. I think I'll have a strong coffee and head back home. You were right, this place isn't good for me."

He'd managed to make me laugh after all.

I mustered my courage and texted Jonah that I needed a one-on-one interview before I could submit my report.

He called a few hours later, sounding concerned and surprised. "I thought we were finished."

I explained he had nothing to fear, this was just a formality, but we needed a concluding interview.

"When?" he asked.

"As soon as possible," I said.

Jonah said they were spending the night by the border fence, but that I could come by the next morning.

I was restless the remainder of the day and could barely sleep that night. I kept startling awake, and at dawn I finally gave up and got dressed. I didn't try to dress younger than my age, nor did I wear my uniform. Instead, I wore a knee-length skirt and a short-sleeved button-down. I added a dainty gold necklace. I tried leather boots. That was a ridiculous choice in this heat, but I hadn't been shoe shopping in a long time. I kept rummaging through my shoe drawer until I found a compromise—open-toed shoes with a low heel.

I left very early, at sunrise, wanting to catch Jonah just as he returned from the border, before he fell asleep. The guard at the gate let me in right away. He remembered me, the lady psychologist from previous visits. I texted Jonah: *I'm here, where are you?*

211

I just came back from a shift, I'm coming to get you, he wrote.

I was worried I'd see him in a different light that morning, but as he emerged from one of the paths he was just as beautiful and sharp as he'd been when we'd lain in the post, and my heart pounded. He said they'd had a busy night. The rioters had hurled a few grenades over the fence and one of our soldiers had gotten injured. "You want to sit at the clubhouse?" he asked.

I told him I'd prefer someplace quiet and suggested his room.

"No problem," he said. "My roommate is home on leave."

I could be wrong about this, I thought. I'd just ask him a few questions and take off.

His room was in one of the bare, mobile cubes that had been placed hastily around base. Inside were two military beds covered with colorful linen brought from home, two metal lockers, an electric kettle, an open package of wafers, a toiletry kit, the smell of men, and Jonah's sniper rifle, chained to the cot with two bolts. "Someone took our chair," he apologized, "so we'll have to sit on the bed, if you don't mind."

"I don't mind," I smiled. We sat close together on his colorful sheet, like teenagers. I was so nervous and insecure that I couldn't remember who was the elder among us, or even how I'd gotten there. But he smelled of shaving cream, all smooth and clean, and I knew what I wanted very badly to do. Then he put his arms around me, I clung to him, and he patiently undid the buttons of my blouse with his gentle fingers.

Like magic, the lesions on my fingers disappeared. My hands were perfect again. *I* was perfect again. I slept well at night and felt relaxed during the day, feeling once more, after all these years, like all options were open and nothing was hindering my path.

But people kept getting in the way. Nivi's mother hyperventilated over the phone as she informed me that he'd been discharged from the hospital and pleaded with me to take him back for therapy. I couldn't believe their gall and said no. I was with the strong guys now, I thought, and this person was dragging me down, accusing me. He had no real desire to be healed. She asked if this was about money and said she was willing to pay extra. I said I didn't want her money.

"Then why?" she asked. "How can you just stop treating him?"

I reminded her of the hospital visit and how they'd both accused me, and said I didn't think we could rebuild the therapeutic bond.

"But you owe him as much," she said, raising her voice. "You did this to him!"

I answered as calmly as a sniper that I wasn't responsible for anything (I imagined she might be recording me) and that I'd done my best to treat him.

"Who's going to take responsibility for him now?" she asked.

"Not me," I answered, and hung up when she started cursing.

A large flock of swifts circled my window, screeching delicately. Someone once told me that these birds never stop flying, even in their sleep. But when the sun set, they vanished among the tree branches and fell silent.

16

IT WAS THE EIGHTH ANNIVERSARY of my mother's death. I picked Dad up, and we stopped on the way to the cemetery to buy a bouquet of sweet peas, her favorite flower.

"Look at my fingers," I said, presenting them to him when we stopped at a light. "They're completely healed."

He was impressed and asked which doctor had treated them.

"I did," I said. "Autosuggestion."

He said he didn't believe it; that the body was much too cunning and powerful for self-healing. He'd forgotten that he'd told me that when my fingers healed I'd know I was on the right track.

"It's a fact," I said, my shooting finger tightening around the steering wheel, remembering the feel of the trigger and of Jonah's gorgeous dick.

There was almost no room left for new dead people at Mom's cemetery. Few funerals were taking place, and the place was silent. Dad sat down to rest on a tombstone near her grave, underneath which a man named Bertie was buried, a small portrait of him adorning the stone. Mom's tombstone was a simple marble plaque engraved with her name and dates of birth and death, without any accompanying epitaph. We lay the bouquet on the grave, and Dad read Mom's favorite poem aloud, "And perhaps it was never so," while I hummed the tune. When I was a child, we would travel in the summertime to a hotel in the Galilee, near Safed. I have an ancient photo from that time of myself running around under pine trees in shorts and sandals while my parents were sprawled in recliners. I imagine Dad was picturing the guesthouses in the European mountains where Jung and Freud would spend their summers. When I got older we stopped going there. Dad didn't like to leave the city and step away from his tiny kingdom, which lay between the front door of the apartment and his clinic.

Dad interrupted my reverie, saying he wanted to be buried underneath Mom, or on top of her, and to have a single tombstone cover both of their bodies. I told him I couldn't care less about my own burial arrangements, and that I'd rather be cremated anyway, because the thought of what went on underneath the dirt made me sick.

"That won't be my responsibility," Dad said. "Talk to your son, it'll be his problem."

It felt good, standing there quietly in the shade with the wind rustling through the tops of the cypress trees. Dad looked very old and infirm. "If you're cremated you won't come back to life during the resurrection," he suddenly said.

I was taken aback.

"Why are you looking at me like that?" he asked. "I prefer the silly beliefs about bodies rising from the dead to your heroic tales of young men descending into an early grave."

I didn't answer. I was done arguing. I had no need for it. "You wanted to say the Kaddish prayer," I reminded him. He recited it by heart, standing up, his Aramaic fluent and precise. "Goodbye, Mom," I said, and all of a sudden I was filled with sorrow for her.

Dad asked me to wait for him at the entrance while he went into the cemetery office to ask about the price of tiered burial. I told him I'd be right back and walked into the clothing store that was peculiarly located right outside the cemetery. It was an upscale, fashionable place selling women's clothing, which thrived thanks to elegant widows' and orphans' lust for life. The boutique owner had craftily hung a little black dress in the store window, the kind one could wear during a mourning period but also for a night out on the town. I asked to try it on and went into the small fitting room. I thought about Rosolio, about Mandy, and about Jonah, wondering which one of them would like it. I looked at myself in the mirror from all directions and walked straight to the cashier to buy it before I could change my mind. I returned to the cemetery office carrying the bag. Dad was sitting there, writing a check for a bearded Chevra Kadisha representative wearing a white shirt and top hat. Dad looked pleased as he limped out of there, leaning on his cane; like a man who'd just cut a profitable deal. "Cheaper than I expected," he said, "and now everything's taken care of. I didn't want it to be a burden on you." I put my arm around him and he leaned against me.

"I bought a dress while you were in there," I said.

"Good," Dad said. "I'm glad you're starting to live." He held on to my hand like a little boy.

Before I had become pregnant, before the idea of having a baby with Rosolio had even crossed my mind, Mom had told me I wasn't delicate enough and that's why I didn't have any suitors. Every week she bought me a different feminine accessory—earrings, perfume, dainty lace blouses—thinking they would help me find a match.

She even gifted me a record of Turkish love songs (her mother was born in Turkey) to teach me what a passionate woman sounded like. Once, she asked me plainly if I didn't like men, and I told her not to be silly. I couldn't explain to her that every time Dad looked at me or her, or spoke to us, I saw in his eyes and heard in his voice that to him women were still only a uterus, hysteria, and penis envy, as stated in the old European books that covered the walls of his clinics, and which were sacred scripture to him. I wanted to rip those books up, to put an end to it all, to create a new psychology—so that he didn't think of me that way.

*

The course I was teaching was coming to an end. I was explaining to the young battalion commanders how to treat survivors of shell shock.

"Finally, something practical," I heard them whispering.

"I need a volunteer," I said.

A few of them raised their hands. I picked an infantry major with a tender face who'd been quiet so far and always seemed to be pondering what I was saying. I called him up onstage. Next, I called up an armored corps officer who liked to talk in class; a chubby, chatty guy. He climbed up onstage with an entertainer's smile. I set the scene: They were soldiers on enemy territory during battle. The armored corps officer has lost control. He just saw a friend being killed and since then has been unresponsive, won't shoot his rifle, won't even duck for cover, won't do anything but pace apathetically. "You need to take care of him," I told the infantry guy. "There are no shrinks, no psychiatrists. The enemy is shooting at you and your friend is out of commission. What do you do?"

The infantry guy looked at the armored corps guy, who had begun playing his role in earnest, and didn't know what to do.

"First of all, take him someplace safe," I instructed. He took the other officer's hand and rushed him off to another corner of the stage. "All right, you're in a sheltered place now. Call him by his name and ask him what's going on. 'What are you feeling? What's wrong? Are you afraid?'"

A few idiotic guffaws sounded in the audience, which were hushed by others.

"I can't take it anymore," the armored corps officer said. "I want to get out of here, I've got to go home, I need my mommy."

"And leave me here alone?" his friend asked him. "How am I supposed to fight them on my own?"

"Run away with me," the shell-shocked one said. "I don't understand what we're doing here. I'm scared of dying."

"They're shooting at you," I said loudly. "The world is falling apart. Shells are falling, grenades are exploding, wounded soldiers are yelling all around you."

"You've got to help me," the infantry guy said. "I can't do this without you."

"He doesn't want to," I intervened. "He wants to defect."

"So what do I do?" he asked awkwardly.

"Tell him to take a deep breath and close his eyes. Calm him down. He's panicked, like prey. His heart rate is too fast. He's hijacked by fear hormones. You need to turn him back into a person again."

"Take a deep breath," he told his friend, holding on to his shoulder. "Close your eyes and think about a song you like. Something quiet. Sing it to yourself."

The armored corps officer obeyed, closing his eyes. The entire room was silent. It was a moment of truth.

"Now put your arms around him," I said.

The two of them stood there, embracing like a couple in the middle of a slow dance. "Let's join the others," the infantry officer told his friend. "We'll finish what we came here to do and get back home alive. Everything is going to be all right. Come with me. I'll keep you safe." He handled the other officer with such natural sweetness that finally his friend raised his head and took hold of his imaginary rifle, prepared to fight, prepared to die.

The two of them walked offstage, arms around each other, one skinny and one chubby, and as they made their way back to their seats the others patted them on their backs and praised them, shooting me appreciative glances for the fine play with the happy ending I'd just put together for them. If only it were that simple in real life.

*

Shauli stood among his friends in the beret ceremony on top of Ammunition Hill, the site of the bloody and glorious battle during the Six-Day War. They had just finished a thirty-seven-mile march. His face was tender and surrounded by an aura of spirituality, like a painting of a Christian martyr. They were all exhausted with effort but kept awake by a sense of elation. "No one could be more beautiful than them," a mother sitting beside me on the bleachers said, beaming.

"You're right," I said, "no one could be more beautiful." I pinched myself against the evil eye and silenced the dark thoughts her statement had inspired.

Since I'd arrived early, I'd had a chance to wander through the trenches along the hill, where the mythological battle had taken place. Now, watching Shauli, I asked myself if he would be able to sacrifice himself in those trenches, charging against hellfire, as he was expected to. All of the symbols, flags, homeland songs, red berets, tears of pride from mothers and brave hugs from fathers were intended to prepare them for that moment of attack, to create a commitment that would prevent them from changing their minds and retreating at the last minute.

The ceremony was understated, the brigade commander's speech short and to-the-point, predictably beginning with the holy battle that had taken place right below us and ending with the challenges we still had to face today. I sat in the bleachers on my own, just like I used to during school plays and birthday parties. I was used to the questioning looks: *Why is she alone? She seems all right, like one of us. Where are her other children, her parents, her husband? What, doesn't her young soldier have a father?* Men looked at me. I attracted them with my solitariness, standing out against the familial goo all around. I was glad I'd brought a light sweater with me because Jerusalem was chilly in the evening. Now the commanders walked among the soldiers, smiling, patting their backs, and placing the red berets atop their shorn heads. The mother next to me began to cry. I felt proud too, but worry trickled through me like poison, overtaking other emotions.

When the ceremony was over I walked down to greet Shauli, struck with awe as I approached him. He let me hold him tightly, his rifle pressing against my ribs. "You did it," I said as I let go.

He smiled awkwardly, an absence in his eyes that I couldn't fill.

"Was the march hard?" I asked.

"Yeah," he said. "We hiked through half the country, but it was beautiful. I'm kind of sorry it's over."

Our surroundings were bustling, families crowding around their heroes, girlfriends kissing and leaning into them; fresh-faced, smiling young girls. The soldiers were new and perfect right now, the red of the berets blending wonderfully with the olive uniform. This wasn't the time to think about what might happen to them later. I considered the many soldiers I'd known during my service. Only a few faces remained in my memory; the rest survived in my mind only as faceless extras standing in threes and quietly carrying out orders.

"What now?" I asked.

The racket continued all around, and Shauli said they were getting a few days' leave and then would be assigned to their battalions. "Why didn't Grandpa come?" he asked, disappointed.

I explained that Grandpa wasn't feeling well and was having trouble walking. That wasn't the whole truth. When Dad had heard the ceremony would be taking place on Ammunition Hill, he'd said he couldn't bear to go to those kinds of places anymore, that they stank of death, and asked me to tell Shauli he missed him.

"You won't make an exception for the boy?" I asked.

He said the best thing we could do for the boy was not to encourage him to die.

One of Shauli's commanders, a young first lieutenant, walked over and patted him hard on the back. Then he looked at me. "Oh, the famous mother! Nice to meet you," he said.

"Famous?" I asked.

He explained that people still talked about me in the brigade—I was the mythological mental health officer.

"I didn't know anyone had figured it out," I said. I was flattered and embarrassed, and I noticed that Shauli was blushing and hiding his face.

"We know everything," the officer said, "and good on

you for carrying on with the heritage." With a satisfied smile, he walked on to greet the next family.

"Do you have any idea what they're saying about me?" I asked Shauli. I felt dizzy and concerned.

He shook his head. He had no idea.

Then we found a quiet corner. I couldn't leave him while all the other families were still there. We edged toward the margins of the revelers. From the side we must have looked like an unpopular child and his doting mother. Occasionally another soldier walked by and high-fived Shauli, but I could tell my son was in a bad mood. I looked around at the other, cheerful families. Compared to them, we looked like we were in mourning.

"Are you tired?" I asked. "Do you think you might be dehydrated?"

He said he'd had plenty of water.

I wondered what might cheer him up, but the only story I could come up with was about how I'd killed a man at the border, and that wasn't something I was allowed to share. "Why are you sad?" I finally asked. I was tired of beating around the bush.

"I'm not sad," Shauli said, lowering his eyes. "I just feel lonely."

"Oh, Shauli." I put my arms around him. I was almost tempted to excuse myself and go call Rosolio and ask him to come meet with us, so that Shauli could have a father here with him after all. When the sun set, the families scattered. I could tell he was dying for me to take him away from there, but I couldn't, it was too late, his game of survival had already begun. "Go be with your friends," I said, offering him the best advice I had to give. "They love you very much. Don't pull away from them. They're your family now."

Commands sounded through the air. The party was over. He got up to join the others.

"Are you all right?" I asked before we said goodbye.

"One hundred percent." He smiled for me, but his eyes remained sad. "I'm over it. Don't worry, everything's fine."

17

COME SEE ME *flying in the Air Force show*, Noga texted me, adding a photo of herself standing next to her chopper, wearing a flight suit and vintage aviator shades, smiling. The kid must be doing all right if she's showing off like this, I thought. Of course I'd go see her.

On Independence Day I made my way toward the beach, walking down the boulevard among throngs of people and stalls selling silly string and plastic flags. I found a corner on a cliff overlooking the beach, slipped on my sunglasses, and looked up at the sky, northward. It was crowded; everyone wanted to come see our power on display. First came a pair of large freight planes with swollen bellies. The crowd applauded. Then we waited for quite a while under an empty sky until a foursome of aerobatic jets appeared, painting loops and lilies of white smoke through the heavens. I held my breath as they descended almost as low as the water before shooting up again. These pilots are so brave, I thought, and must be so mentally balanced to keep their concentration and not crash into the audience or the water. Another break. I'd once taken Shauli to watch this air show when he was little, but the sunlight had been harsh and he'd had trouble looking up at the sky. When the fighter jets approached with a roar he cried out with fear, and we'd never attended again. But soon Noga would appear in the sky, and she'd asked me to come see her.

Someone touched my shoulder. I turned around and was surprised to find Mandy's daughter with her husband and two children, her face kind and plump, smiling. She introduced me to her husband, who shook my hand. There was power in this family portrait. I was happy to see her so together while I was looking desolate on that cliff, waiting for the cavalry to stride in. "Hi, kids," I said, then added with a kind of apology, "my son is a big boy now." Just then, I heard the rattling of choppers and looked up so as not to miss them. Three flying fortresses, their metal bodies twisted at an angle like complicated origami. One of them was piloted by Noga. I imagined the focused expression on her face and the healthy, shining hair pinned up underneath her helmet, the sensitive fingers operating the machinery, and heard the boyish voice speaking softly over the radio with the other pilot. I held my breath. They flew as steadily as otherworldly dragons. The audience around me went wild, clapping as if the pilots were able to hear them up there. I joined in on their enthusiasm, waving at the sky without embarrassment or guilt. It was a moment of pure pride. But the choppers disappeared southward quickly, to another city, vanishing from view. I looked behind me for Mandy's daughter, wanting to see her face and her family again, glad she'd approached me rather than hold a grudge. I must have helped her a little bit after all. But they'd moved on. Silence returned to the beach, but only for a moment, because just then a triplet of fighter jets emerged with a terrible rumble and one of them suddenly ascended on its own to the apex of the sky, reaching almost all the way to the sun.

I walked back into town through the crowd. I texted Noga that I'd seen her, that I was proud of her, that she was wonderful. She texted back a heart and wrote, *Thank you for everything*, then added a kiss.

Jonah came over in the late afternoon, once Independence Day was over. Another team of snipers had taken over the border post, and he'd gotten leave for the holiday. Jonah looked around my apartment with his pale green gaze, including me in it as well. I'd put on tight jeans and a cute T-shirt for him. Shauli didn't get leave, so we had the place to ourselves. In civilian clothing Jonah looked even younger and skinnier than he did in uniform. He'd borrowed his parents' car and driven almost two hours to see me. I asked if he wanted to take a walk and was relieved when he said no. How would I have explained him out on the street? I asked him to talk to me for a bit, I wanted to hear his voice. The holiday hubbub had died down and only the swifts circled and squawked through the air in twilight madness.

"What do you want me to say?"

"Tell me what you did last night."

"I went to the outdoor stages in our village," he said obediently. "There were no famous singers, only local amateurs. And a dance troupe. I was with my little brothers—I have two. Then they went over to see their friends and I walked around on my own for a while. I ran into people I know and they shook my hand. They know what I do in the military and respect me for it. Everyone keeps praising me. Then I looked for the caramel apple guy. That's my favorite thing on Independence Day. But he wasn't there this year, I don't know why, and that was sort of disappointing. So I walked out of the village and down the road, alongside the woods. I wanted some quiet. I saw the fireworks over our village. After that I went back home and got into bed. In the morning you texted me to come over, and now I'm here."

"Why did you come?" I asked. I persisted even though he was surprised by the question. "What is it you want from me?"

I was testing him. He looked around the room like an alley cat trapped in a strange home and seeking an escape route. "Because I feel like being with you," he said. "I don't have another reason."

That was good enough for me. I could have searched for other, more sophisticated explanations about a sex drive or a death wish or a mother complex, or about the bond we'd forged when we'd squeezed the trigger together, but I didn't want to be too smart about it. He felt good with me. That was enough. "All right, you can be with me," I said.

He got up and came to sit with me on the couch. I rested his childish head against my shoulder and his hand in my lap. The sun had set, but I didn't turn on the light. The holiday was over. He turned his face to kiss me. His mouth tasted sweet and his hand settled in my lap.

Suddenly I had an idea. "Come on," I said. I gave him my hand and led him down the hallway to the clinic.

"What's this?" he asked.

"This is where I work," I said, "and now this is where we're going to be together." I shut the door as if he'd come for a therapy session, but only turned on the reading lamp on the desk. I undressed in front of him, pants, shirt. I was wearing cute little underwear and the dim lighting disguised everything I didn't like to show. Our shadows loomed large against the bookcase. "Have a seat, Jonah," I said, pointing at my chair. Then I kneeled before him, naked.

*

Dad's hospitalization caught me in a gray, suburban hotel on a continuing education day, hosted by the military's Mental Health Branch and attended by over a hundred mental health officers from all over the military. I was explaining how to prepare soldiers to charge and win while also treating those who suffered trauma without pausing the attack. This was a major shift in perception and some people voiced their objections, but most of them happily accepted the refreshing change. They too wanted to be a part of victory. Only when we broke for lunch did I see that Dad had called me a few times. I called him back right away, but he didn't pick up. I dialed his number again and again until a strange woman's voice answered.

"I'm a nurse," she said. "He was admitted here." She explained that an ambulance had brought him to the hospital.

"What happened?" I asked, "Is he all right?"

"He's obviously not all right," she scolded, "or else he wouldn't have been hospitalized. But he can talk. Would you like to speak to him?"

"What happened, Dad?" I asked.

He answered meekly that he hadn't been feeling well and had collapsed at home. The paramedics had to break the door down because he couldn't get up to open it. "Where were you? Why didn't you pick up?" Dad asked. I explained. He could understand.

"Are you feeling better now?" I asked.

"Connected to tubes. That's exactly what I didn't want. I don't want it to end like this. Bring the thing in the envelope I showed you. I want to have it with me."

"I'll come by as soon as I can," I said, not perceiving him to be in any imminent danger.

"Come, Abigail!" Dad sounded scared. "I don't want to be alone here. They'll take over soon."

But I couldn't just stop the workshop halfway through. It had been so difficult to get all the mental health officers from all military units to the same place at the same time, and this refresher course was vital for what was on the horizon. "I'll come a little later, Dad," I said, "as soon as I can."

I was at my finest that day, offering them my knowledge and experience. I didn't just convey information—I broke through the barriers in their minds. I was once again the gifted child who stunned everybody with the force of a killer. We finished our concluding discussion that afternoon, and as I gathered my things and hurried out to go see Dad, I heard the Combat Engineering Corps' mental health officer saying to a colleague, "When will robots finally replace those poor kids so we can stop ruining their lives?" She was a gentle, serious young woman who reminded me of myself when I first started. I liked her, but I couldn't keep quiet about that remark. I talked back to her in front of everybody; it was important to me that they all hear it: "People will fight forever. War is part of nature, and robot operators also have souls that need to be considered. Our duty is to treat them and help them win."

"Just help them, you mean. Winning has nothing to do with our role. We need to keep them sane," she said.

She was wearing dainty glasses and simple earrings. She'd decided to argue with me now.

"You're wrong," I said. "It's our role to help them win."

She huffed in silence, gazing at me with hostility, as if I were a traitor to my profession. I could understand where she was coming from. I'd been through all of those dilemmas over the years, and now they were over. "Nothing is more damaging to a soldier's mental health than defeat," I said with the sort of calm and authority that did not tolerate objection. "That's why, this time, we're finally going to help them win." Then, charging the air around me with electricity, I said, "And another thing. They aren't kids. Calling them that is disrespectful. Stop calling them kids."

Dad was dying, his eyes wandering through other realms. I saw it as soon as I walked in. He was lying in the farthest of three beds, tubes poking out from all over him.

"Dad." I was startled. I hadn't realized things were this bad. He was sighing, trying to focus his blurry eyes on me. "I'm sorry I only got here now. I couldn't leave earlier, and you said . . ." I took his limp hand; it was skin and bones.

"Abigail," he said meekly, "where's Shauli?"

"Shauli's in the army," I said. "He might come home on Saturday."

"I want to see him," he said. "I don't have much time left."

"I don't know if—"

"Get Shauli over here."

I looked for a doctor to try and assess the situation. I found the doctor on call, who said the tests showed that Dad's disease had become very advanced, which is why he'd collapsed that morning.

"How much time does he have?" I asked.

"Little," he said. "We'll do everything we can, but I've got to level with you: this is the end of the road."

"Because, you see, I have a kid in the military, his grandson, and he wants to see him. What I'm asking is, does the situation justify getting him to ask for leave."

"I don't know," the doctor said matter-of-factly. "That's your call."

"Is he in a lot of pain?" I asked.

The doctor said he was getting morphine and anything else that could alleviate the pain. No need for cyanide, then, I thought. I could save that for my own plan.

I returned to Dad's bedside. "What are you thinking, Dad?" I asked.

"I'm scared, Abigail," he said. "Don't leave me."

I wanted to dim the light, which was too bright, but the switch only allowed for complete light or total darkness, and when I turned it off someone in another bed protested. "Light!" another dying man cried. "Bring back the light!" I turned it back on.

"I spoke to Shauli," I lied. "He'll be here tomorrow morning."

Dad smiled contentedly and fell asleep. I looked at him with sorrow, not crying, until my eyelids drooped with exhaustion and I dozed off uncomfortably on the chair. Suddenly it occurred to me that I hadn't talked to him enough, and that if he died right now I wouldn't have another opportunity. I tried to rouse him. "Dad, wake up," I said softly, "I need to ask you something." But his mind was too foggy to answer.

In the middle of the night I startled awake when his monitor started beeping. Dad wasn't breathing. I hurried into the hallway to get a doctor, and the staff rushed in and tried to revive him. After some effort, they dropped their instruments and turned off the machines, their apologetic, defeated eyes telling me they'd failed; that they'd never stood a chance.

Dad was buried the next afternoon. They removed the tombstone and buried him on top of Mom, just as he'd wanted. I'd posted a small obituary in the newspaper so that he didn't leave this world without a single mention.

Our beloved, I wrote on top, and *the grieving family* at the bottom. I smiled to myself. Shauli and I stood over the grave beside Dad's elderly cousin whom I hadn't seen in years, two retired professors from the psychology department, and a few other people I didn't know, perhaps patients or colleagues. The small size of the gathering seemed inappropriate for making speeches, and Shauli didn't want to say anything either. He'd arrived straight from base, with his uniform and rifle. For some reason, I kept expecting Rosolio to show up too, but the paths remained still, no entourage in olive uniforms materializing.

We sat shiva at my parents' apartment. Shauli received three days' leave. That's what military procedures dictated when grandparents pass away. Had I died, he would have gotten seven days. Only a few condolence callers came by, but it was a good time for me and Shauli. We had some peace and quiet, ate all of our meals together, spoke about my father and mother. Shauli had many happy memories with them. They'd loved him so much. When we came home from the funeral he cried and let me hold him. I also wept intensely throughout the first night. Then we stopped. We pulled out my parents' photo albums. There weren't many of them. I interpreted old pictures for Shauli, presenting him with this documentation from different moments of their lives. Not everything I could explain. I only dared set foot in Dad's clinic two days later, entering the holiest of holies. I debated what to do with all his old books that I had no need for, which were filled with outdated theories that I hated.

Some of Dad's old patients came by to mourn with us. I recognized them by the hesitant way they entered the room. "Please come in," I said, greeting them. They praised him gently, telling us how he'd helped them and lent an ear for years. I looked at their body language and listened to their intonations, recognizing all the old neuroses they hadn't recovered from and that couldn't be cured, testing Dad's product like a craftsman. Some of my gifted classmates from school came by, too. I introduced them to Shauli, showing him off. They told the story of a birthday party Mom had once thrown for me in this apartment, and how Dad had tried to screen cartoons against a sheet on the wall, but the projector didn't work, and how I was so disappointed that he tried to make it up to me with some magic trick but couldn't pull that off either. "Poor thing, I forgot all about that," I said, laughing. A realtor who'd seen the obituary also stopped by, shamelessly asking what I planned to do with the apartment and offering his services.

Mandy came on the second day—I'd given him the news late. He cooked us fresh food and spent a long time talking with Shauli in the dining area. I listened in from a distance. Shauli quietly told him everything he wouldn't tell me, about their nighttime operations, how they invaded people's houses, searched them, and arrested people in their beds. I was surprised by his flowing confession. Mandy listened, occasionally interjecting with brief, plain questions. He wanted to know if they were met with a lot of resistance, and Shauli said that typically everything went smoothly. They detained the wanted person without a hitch. Sometimes a wife or mother started yelling or the kids woke up. It was unpleasant, but one got used to it. Mandy listened without expressing opinions or voicing criticism. I envied him. I should have been the one listening to Shauli's story.

The entire time, my ears were pricked for Noga's light footsteps on the stairs or the heavy tread of Rosolio and his guards. The other, mundane mourners trickled in, sat down, said a few words. Sometimes I had brief conversations with them, but other times I couldn't be bothered. Halfway through the shiva I couldn't help it anymore and texted Noga: *My father died*. I waited a few minutes, picturing her advanced mind grinding through the information and considering how to respond. I could practically see the neurons linking feverishly inside the gray matter.

Abigail, I'm so sorry, she texted. *Can I come over?*

When she came by the next day, only Shauli and I were home. We'd run out of condolence callers. Noga stood in the doorway like a wish come true. I hugged and kissed her and invited her inside. Shauli came out of his room to greet her and they acknowledged each other with the indifference of young people. I asked if she was hungry. It was lunchtime and she'd told me she'd requested special permission to leave the squadron. I set a plate of Mandy's leftover stew in front of her and she ate voraciously. I explained that this was the apartment where I'd grown up, and she asked if she could see my old room. "Of course," I said, and led her there. The room remained as it had been years ago when I'd moved out. A twin bed covered with an Indian tapestry I'd bought at the flea market, in no way fit for two people (I'd never spent the night with anyone here), the desk I'd had since elementary school, a bookcase, and a dusty tape deck. On the wall, a pretty and melancholic oil painting hung, depicting a thicket and the side of a mountain. Dad had gotten it as a gift from his artist patient and couldn't find a better spot for it. I sat on the old bed, pulled my knees into my chest. I was sad in there, and Noga put her arms around me. I spotted Shauli standing awkwardly in the doorway, ready to flee. "Come in," I told him. The three of us sat on the narrow bed in my old room. I was happy to be there with both of them, though they were years too late. I noticed Shauli watching Noga, charmed. He'd discovered her. She smiled at him and treated him with the tenderness of an older sister.

Noga got up to leave, saying she had to get back to the squadron.

"Hang on, Noga, I've got something for you," I said. "Come with me." I took her to Dad's clinic. She looked around curiously. "Don't worry, this won't hurt." I explained that this was where Dad used to see his patients, asked her to have a seat, and pulled out the old manila envelope from the desk drawer.

"What's this?" she asked.

"This is for you," I said, fishing out the tiny metal shell with the tips of my fingers. "This used to belong to my father, and now it's yours. There's poison inside that kills you instantly. From now on you don't have to be afraid anymore. Take good care of it, and they'll never catch you alive. You're free now."

"That's it?" Noga laughed, startled. "This can replace all of our talking? It's that easy?"

"Now we can talk only about happy things." I smiled.

She folded the envelope and slipped it into her pocket. "Why did your father have poison in his desk?"

"It's part of the aging psychologist's survival kit. Freud kept one in his desk drawer and everyone else copied him," I lied.

"Sure, why not," she said with a smile. "Thank you for thinking of me. It would be cool to die by poison, very retro."

"You're not going to die," I said softly. "You're strong. Treat it like a good luck charm. And here's another." I removed a gold chain with a ruby pendant from my neck. I didn't want to be associated in her mind only with death. "This is also for you." She was very moved. I could see her beautiful jugular pounding as I clasped the chain around her neck. Then she fell into my arms. I rubbed her hair and sent her off on her way.

Jonah came on the last day of the shiva. The apartment was empty, even Shauli had returned to base by that point. I led Jonah into my old room and we lay in my childhood bed from evening till morning, until we'd obliterated the stale odor of virginity from it. The next day, after he left, I spent a long time sitting by the desk in Dad's clinic, reading through the index cards he'd kept on all his patients over the years, written in his careful hand.

He wrote well about them, with wisdom and astuteness. Many of them were long dead. I dug through their souls in those cards until I'd had enough. When darkness fell and the clinic was filled with deathly silence I began to tear the cards up. I tore them to shreds, one by one, my eyes occasionally falling on a line in which Dad had sentenced the fate of a patient. I mixed up the shreds and divided them between several trashcans along the street, as if disposing of criminal evidence.

After the shiva was over, I went to visit Mandy in his village. I planned to stay there until further notice. I informed my patients I was taking some time off. When I arrived I asked that we refrain from discussing death or the military. "Put me to work," I said.

Mandy said he truly did need help. All of the figs were ripening at once and had to be picked quickly. The pomegranates had to be wrapped in paper to protect them from pecking birds. A new irrigation system had to be installed in the olive grove. He had been planning on hiring a laborer to help him, but would prefer to have me. I worked in the intense summer heat in shorts, a wide-brimmed hat, and his wife's old work boots. My muscles ached, but my mind was calm and clear. I focused on the branches from which I picked the fruit and on the dirt on which I laid the hoses, barely thinking about anything else. The sun darkened my skin to near-black. Mandy liked it, and would touch me every evening until I fell asleep. I left my phone in a remote corner of the house and tried to check it as rarely as possible, briefly glancing at it every few hours just to check if Shauli or Noga had called.

One night, Mandy yelled in his sleep. When I shook him awake I was almost tempted to tell him I'd killed a man too, and look, I was dealing with it just fine, no nightmares. Though my life had changed, gaining added meaning and depth, I hardly even thought about the guy I'd killed. I never tried to learn his name or find out his story. But I resisted the urge and said nothing. Now I had two eternal secrets I carried around inside of me, like babies who would never be born.

That night, in the studio, Mandy decided he was tired of me watching him work, and placed a damp, brown lump of clay in front of me. "Here, do something with this," he said.

I buried my hands in the clay. The slipperiness repelled and attracted me all at once. I played with it, beginning to form a small person—head, neck, shoulders, torso. I kept changing the genitals from male to female. I couldn't make up my mind.

"Keep going, this is interesting," Mandy said from a distance. He was busy with his own iron sculptures, welding and breaking the material. His hair and beard had grown wild, and he offered me a kind smile I didn't deserve.

I wanted to stay much longer, but the rumble of war had begun. "Listen," Mandy said. Normally, all we could hear at night was the howling of jackals and the wind, but now the relative quiet was disrupted by a dull thumping, as if enormous iron balls were hitting the ground. Then the growling of fighter jets started and didn't stop. "Something's going on," Mandy said.

I thought about Shauli, who hadn't spoken to me in a long time, and whom I might have neglected for the sake of my peace of mind. I got out of bed tensely, my slow pulse quickening, and like an addict falling off the wagon I grabbed my phone and looked through all the news websites. I sat down in the kitchen (which still contained traces of Mandy's wife, old recipes in her handwriting filling the drawers) and waited for morning. I knew it was beginning.

The next morning, we insisted on working the farm as if nothing was happening, even though we could hear distant sirens, followed by enemy barrages. Missiles and counter-missiles flew through the sky as in a deranged science fiction movie. We were almost finished wrapping the pomegranates and laying the new irrigation system, and Mandy was asking me to shear stray branches, showing me the right way to do it. I heard my phone wailing from inside the house. Somebody wanted very badly to speak with me. I hurried inside.

"Come," Rosolio's office manager said into the phone, her voice urgent.

"Now?" I asked.

"Yes, if you can," she said. "That's what he asked me to tell you. Call when you get here and I'll make sure they let you in."

When I returned to the orchard, Mandy could see it on me. He read me well. "Are you happy your war is starting?"

I'd forgotten to wipe the little smile off my lips. Rosolio still needed me. I told Mandy I had to go, that I'd been called to duty. I quickly changed my clothes, sprayed myself with deodorant, said goodbye to Mandy, and drove madly back into town. I tried to get a hold of Shauli along the way, but he didn't pick up. I turned on the radio after so many days away and heard some of the blather. The talk show hosts were wondering out loud if we were going to win this time or if this was going to be another war that amounted to nothing, just like last time and the time before that. I turned it off. I despised people who were all talk. Talk is cheap. From the news reports, I gathered that the big fire had yet to be lit.

18

MANY MILES BEFORE reaching the city, I was met with the usual traffic and had to go off-road and overtake it from the shoulder. If a cop pulled me over, I'd show my military officer ID and explain that the Chief of Staff was expecting me.

Rosolio's office manager had sent a young second lieutenant to wait for me at the gate, and he got me quickly through all the checkpoints until we walked into the high command underground war room. I was met with a wave of cold air. Rows and rows of pale soldiers were sitting in front of screens as a soft electronic beeping sounded in the background. There was no way to tell if it was day or night outside. This was only a simulacrum of reality. The officer led me into a side room at the edge of a skywalk, illuminated by blinding lights, and asked me to wait. I looked at my hands, which were scratched from working with Mandy but beautiful and healthy, not a lesion in sight. I spread them over the desk proudly. I waited a long time, until a tumult started in the hallway. His bodyguards had arrived, looking over the room, including me, as if I were just a part of the architecture. Rosolio walked in after them. He seemed trapped among them, his head lowered with worry and his footsteps heavy. The guards waited outside, by the door. Only the two of us were in the room, sitting at a bare desk alongside dim screens.

"You look like you just came back from summer camp," Rosolio said. "It's good to know there's a life outside of this place. It's easy to forget that in here."

"Why did you call me in?" I asked.

Rosolio said a decision had been made to launch the real war tomorrow. This time, we were going all the way. Not only an aerial attack, not only a navy attack, but a land attack as well. Large forces would invade, with the purpose of conquering and winning.

"All right," I said, waiting for him to offer me an opening.

"The plans are ready," he said. "Every unit knows what it has to do. We've been very organized since I took on the role."

I sat before him, erect, self-assured, and said, "Excellent."

He leaned over the desk and looked around to make sure nobody was listening in or reading his lips. Here it comes, I thought.

"Abigail," Rosolio said, "my heart is heavy, there's a weight on my chest. I've been having a recurring nightmare about going out to battle with a large army, horses, swords, flags, and trumpets, but then everybody disappears and it's just me and the enemy."

I knew what he was like in these kinds of situations; knew it as well as the back of my hand. But now we didn't have enough time, and the responsibility was immense. "Give me your hand," I said.

He obeyed and offered his closed fist.

"Let go, Rani, loosen up," I said, rubbing his palm. "Close your eyes, Rani." I knew his entire history, and how his mind worked, and I knew this was what he needed now, not an outpouring of words. I had to block the fear mechanism that had taken over him, remove the weight from his chest, and imbue him with confidence. "Close your eyes," I said again, putting my two hands, which still contained the warmth of the earth, on the sides of his face. "You've got to get out of here," I said quietly. "You can't run a war exclusively from this bunker. This place is diminishing you with cold and concern. Get a chopper tomorrow and travel between the units. Let them see you."

"I have to stay here, how can I leave?" Rosolio said with his eyes closed. He was giving himself over to me and I felt I could do with him as I pleased. The guards were outside the room and the glass was soundproof. "Fly out for just a few hours, then come back here."

"All right," he said, nodding hard. "That's what I'll do." His eyes remained closed and I rubbed his hair with my perfect hand. When he got up he ran his hand down my cheek, and had I let him he would have kissed me with gratitude as well, but I didn't need it. "Now go win," I said. He walked out to meet his bodyguards.

Shauli called and said they'd been given two minutes to speak to their mothers. What could I ask him in a moment like that? How he felt? Whether he was afraid? Or was it best just to tell him how much I loved him? I wanted him to go into battle independent and strong, annihilate the enemy, and get out alive. I didn't want him to even think about me. In my mind, I heard the awful cries of the dying that my fighters had told me about. "Mommy! Mommy!" I had to move away from that place, so I asked silly questions, like if they had enough food—he said they did—and if it was very hot, as if I didn't know the answer to that. I thought about the pale soldiers sitting in front of their screens in the bunker, safe from harm, and how Shauli could have been sitting with them, watching it all unfold from afar, if it hadn't been for the poisonous enthusiasm I'd injected into him. Shauli said he had to go, that his time was up.

"Don't be afraid to shoot, Shauli," I told him just before he hung up. We could deal with the repercussions later, as long as he got out of there alive.

The radio reported that the war had begun, but the city was unimpressed. It was as if nobody's children were serving in the military. I walked outside because I couldn't stay home with my worries. The cafes were full of people, their mouths moving nonstop, eating and talking. They reminded me of rats, motivated only by food and sex. I was sorry I wasn't on the front lines with the soldiers. I would have fought alongside them fearlessly, down to the final bullet. I was sure of it. Instead, I was stuck at home, turning the TV prattle on and off, praying not to hear heavy footsteps climbing up the stairs, bringing me a terrible announcement.

At some point, a woman called and introduced herself as one of Dad's old patients. She'd only just found out he'd died, because she'd been out of the country, and wanted to extend her sympathies. "Every week," she said, "for twenty-two years, I came to see him. That man kept me alive. He meant so much to me. I could see him growing gaunt and frail, I guess he was sick, but to me he was like a rock. I wanted to tell him about my trip. What am I going to do now? Who's going to help me?"

What's wrong with these people? I wondered. Then an odd idea occurred to me. "Listen," I said, "I'm also a clinical psychologist. I'm seeing patients. If it's urgent, maybe you could come in for a session and we can see if it's a fit."

She jumped at my offer. "That would be wonderful. If you've inherited even a smidgeon of his brilliance, that would be more than enough for me. Could I come in this afternoon?"

"Why not," I said, "I'll see you at Dad's clinic." That was a good way to pass the time and alleviate some of my anxiety.

I went to my parents' apartment, cleaned up the mess of the shiva, and aired the space out. I was sorry I'd thrown out all of Dad's notes. Now I knew nothing about this lady who was coming in for a session and I'd have to start fresh.

She was punctual. I greeted her at the door, just like Dad used to, and led her into the clinic. A good-looking woman, older than I was, around sixty, a nice body, fine clothes, dainty gold jewelry dotted with small gems. "Have a seat," I said, "you know the drill." I sat down in Dad's chair.

"This is a little strange," she said awkwardly. "Where should I begin?"

"From the beginning. I don't know anything about you."

"Oh," she laughed, "so that's how years of talking go down the drain? Do you have any idea how many tears I've cried in this room? Is there really nothing left?"

"You're left," I said. She smiled. There was a lot I wanted to ask her about Dad and what he was like as a therapist, but I held back.

"It's going to be long, and my life isn't very interesting," she said. "I used to discuss my little problems with your father. I wasn't embarrassed. I talked about fights with my husband, about my children, about people who mistreated me at work, little insults, that sort of childish thing. We talked a lot about my parents, even though they'd already died. Where should I start?"

"Tell me about your week," I said. "We can start there." I leaned back to listen. She was nice to look at, and I had to pass the time somehow. But halfway through the session, when she was telling me about an embarrassing incident during a work meeting abroad that was preoccupying her, I spotted a text from Noga on my phone. Finally. I'd been trying to get a hold of her for days. "Excuse me for one moment," I told Dad's patient.

I read Noga's message: *Madness, a perfect amusement park, I feel good*, it said. I texted back right away, *My hero, give them hell and keep us safe.*

"I apologize," I told the patient, who was gaping at me. That kind of thing would have never happened with Dad. The whole country could burn down and he still wouldn't pick up his phone in the middle of a session. "My daughter," I explained with a smile. "She's in the military. She just texted to say she was fine."

"Oh," the patient said empathetically. Her fingers were playing with the gold chain around her neck. She kept talking.

Then Noga texted a gorgeous photo of herself in a flight suit and dark glasses, her chopper tall and angular behind her. I held the phone close to my eyes to check out her smile. It was real. Then I held the picture to my lips. I'd done well with this sweet girl. Let's just hope she does well in battle. I returned my eyes to this woman and her troubles. "Please carry on," I said. "You were talking about embarrassment."

Two days later, I got a call in the afternoon from an unfamiliar number. I was a little sleepy, having taken a Valium a day, half in the morning and half at night. When I picked up, startled, a young woman said my name.

"I'm from your son's battalion," she said, "from the adjutant's office. I'm in the gathering area and I think you should come here. They just got a few hours' break, and he isn't okay. I'm not supposed to talk to you, but he asked me to."

"Wait a second," I said, "what do you mean he isn't okay? Is he hurt? Is he alive?"

"Listen, I'm not supposed to even be talking to you," she repeated. "He's alive, he isn't wounded, but he isn't okay, you know? He wants his mother, that's the only thing he keeps saying, so I called you. That's it, I've got to go now."

"Wait, don't hang up," I pleaded. "Where are you exactly?"

She gave me the location, speaking quickly and swallowing her words, but I figured it out, more or less. Then she hung up.

I walked out the door and into my car right away, driving to Shauli through a series of sirens. The radio reported collapsing buildings and people being killed, but I wasn't afraid. There was a crisis and I had to handle it. I'd been preparing for this moment from the day Shauli had enlisted, knowing deep inside that it would arrive. I made sure to put on my uniform because I knew I'd have to demonstrate authority. And indeed, close to the eucalyptus thicket where the battalion was deployed, near the border, I was stopped by a military cop who asked where I was headed. I told him I was a military psychologist summoned to join the battalion. He saw my insignia and let me through.

I looked for Shauli's company in the staging area. Soldiers were conducting roll call in preparation to reenter the battlefield, but he wasn't among them. Equipment and ammunition crates were scattered around, armored vehicles crossing the area, raising dust clouds. Cooks were setting a table of sliced bread, jam, and hard-boiled eggs. Had I not been searching for my son within this chaos I might have enjoyed myself; I loved this energy. Eventually I found him leaning against a tree trunk. They'd been fighting for three days with hardly any sleep and were now on a short break till nightfall, when they would be going back in. Everyone around him was lost in desperate sleep, but Shauli's eyes were open, his gaze distant and gauzy.

"Shauli," I whispered, moving toward him quietly.

"Mom," he said, standing up, like a child whose mother was late to pick him up from kindergarten. "Let's get out of here."

I put my arms around him and he remained frozen in place, his arms drooping by his body. "Let's sit down, Shauli, I want to talk. Look at me for a moment," I said.

"Let's go home, let's leave," he said decisively.

I could tell he was deep inside a dark well. How would I get him out of there? "You want to tell me what happened?" I asked.

"No," he said, panicking, shaking his head hard.

"Oh, so you're his mother." A young man's voice sounded behind us. "I'm the company commander." His face was strewn with dark stubble. He said, "He had a bit of a hard time inside and we helped him out, just like we were taught. I think he should be fine by tonight. We didn't lose a single soldier, only three injured, and that's the most important thing. We killed quite a few of theirs. Shauli fought perfectly until he started having a hard time. I understand you're an expert in this, but it isn't very convenient for us to have you here right now. Our mental health officer is treating other cases and will get to him soon. We ought to do this in an organized way. It's our responsibility, and you can rest assured we're taking good care of him."

"What exactly happened out there?" I asked. The officer's face was covered with soot, bloodstains on his uniform. He hadn't had a chance to wash up in the water containers laid across the field for them. He said, "War, you know, unpleasant things. Very ugly."

"Mom, I want to go," Shauli murmured, holding my hand. He was dirty and smelled.

I asked the commander if there was a clean change of

uniform for my son, and he said they'd take care of that later, there were some more urgent matters to attend to. He stood next to us, expecting me to leave, but I couldn't leave Shauli like that. "Listen," I said, "let me speak to the battalion commander." But the company commander said the battalion commander was on the battlefield with the forces and could not be contacted.

"I want to take him someplace quiet for a few hours. I'll take care of him. This is my profession. I'll bring him back before nightfall. All right?"

The company commander glanced around at his sleeping soldiers, pondering this. "They'll ask where he disappeared to," he said. "I can't have a march of defectors here. You see, the initial enthusiasm is gone, after three days they've gotten the gist of it and nobody really wants to go back in, but we've got no choice. I can't give him special treatment."

"Do you really think he can go back inside in his current state?" I asked.

"I do," he confirmed. "This is no time for pampering. I need every single infantryman. I don't have any excess manpower. He'll go inside with us, and come out with us, and we'll take care of him later."

That's what happened to Nivi, I thought, when I sent him back in, not letting him get soft. But this time it was my son. "All I'm asking you is for two or three hours," I said. "It's two o'clock now, I'll get him back by five."

"Mom, don't bring me back," Shauli screeched.

The company commander looked at me and my insignia and said, "Listen, I want to help you out, but he's got to be back here by five, not a minute later. I'm trusting you here. If anyone asks, I'm going to say he's with the mental health officer. At five o'clock I want you to bring him back, good as new, you hear?"

"Fine," I said. "Trust me." I dragged Shauli quickly to the car. There was no time to go home, and I knew if I took him there I wouldn't be able to bring him back, anyway. I called Mandy, who lived thirty minutes away, and told him we were on our way.

The radio in the car was playing the news, and I switched it to music and looked at Shauli, who didn't seem to be hearing a thing.

"What was the hardest part?" I asked. He didn't answer. His soul was crushed and he couldn't carry on a simple conversation. "Where's your rifle?" I asked.

He flinched, looking all around him and underneath his seat. "Lost," he said. "Go back, Mom, the rifle is lost."

I pulled up and called the number the company commander had given me. He said Shauli had left his rifle by the tree and that they were holding on to it for him.

"Get him back here on time," he told me again. "I don't want any trouble."

Mandy heard the car approach and stepped outside to greet us. When I got out of the car with Shauli I didn't have to explain a thing. We had to get him cleaned up, but I was worried he might hurt himself if I left him alone in the bathroom. "I'll stand outside the door and listen," Mandy whispered.

"Go take a shower, Shauli," I said softly. "You'll feel better."

"What do I do with him now?" I asked Mandy outside the bathroom door.

He said, "I'll help you with whatever you decide, but I can't make the decision for you."

I had all sorts of extreme ideas on how to smuggle him out, images of the Mediterranean Sea and the hull of a boat where I would stash him. I got a hold of myself; took a deep breath. When Shauli was all cleaned up, wearing shorts and a shirt that Mandy had given him and that were too big, I sat him down, made him an omelet, chopped some vegetables, and sliced some bread. He ate passionately, which was a good sign. Maybe after he got some food and sleep in him he'd wake up refreshed. This might be just a physiological matter of hunger and fatigue. But he wouldn't speak.

"What happened out there?" I asked, but he just shook his head and kept eating. "Shauli, how do you feel?" He looked at me again with that frightening, unfocused gaze of a person whose mind has suffered a terrible beating. I asked myself, *If he were just another soldier in the battalion, not your son, how would you treat him right now?* I would have left him back there, among his friends, and had them try to get him talking and give him some strength before going back onto the battlefield. That's what our procedure dictated.

"I think you should get some sleep," I said. "We can talk when you wake up. You're very tired." It had been over an hour since I'd taken him away from the staging area, and time was running out. I don't know what exactly I was thinking, taking him out of there. I guess I'd been hoping for a miracle. Mandy quickly made up the living room sofa and lowered the blinds. Shauli lay down and I covered him with a blanket. I watched his eyeballs moving restlessly underneath the lids. My eyes closed for a moment, but then I recalled with a start that I still had to wash his uniform. I couldn't send him back there in soiled gear. Maybe that could be an excuse to keep him here, I could say he didn't have a clean uniform. My thoughts were getting frazzled. Mandy stood behind me in the bathroom while I scrubbed the clothes and spoke to me through the mirror. "I can solve this," he said, "if you let me."

"How?"

"With this." He held up a small, very sharp knife he used for cutting iron in his studio.

"What's that for?"

"Cutting off the tip of his shooting finger, that's all," he said. "It'll hurt, but I can clean and dress the wound and give him a strong painkiller. It'll start healing within a couple of days, he won't even need to go to the hospital. He can't fight without a shooting finger. He'd be useless to them."

That was pretty shocking. I had to process the idea. "I don't know," I said, tempted.

"We've got to do it now," Mandy said, "before your time runs out."

Through the mirror, my hands submerged in water and detergent, I asked, "Why didn't you do it to yourself when you were his age?"

"Shauli wouldn't do it to himself either. I'd do it for him. And don't forget: there's a big difference between us. I loved to kill, he doesn't. He's too tender. He isn't built for war. Just look at him sleeping there like a baby bird."

I hung the uniform out to dry out on the clothing line and returned to the dim room where Shauli slept. I was exhausted and out of sorts. "Under no circumstances can you cut his finger without my permission," I told Mandy, then paced back and forth, unable to make up my mind. I was sorry Dad wasn't alive. I could have called him, he would have helped me. What's the value of everything you've learned, I asked myself, and what good are your many years of military service, if you don't know how to save your own son?

"Ortal, Chief of Staff Office Manager," my screen read when my phone started ringing, and I quickly stepped outside.

"Abigail," his office manager said, "he wants to talk to you."

I glanced at my watch. Too much time had passed, and the leave we'd been given was running out. I waited for Rosolio to get on the line.

"Abigail, what's this I'm hearing about the boy?" he demanded without any introductions.

My breath caught. How the hell did he know about it? "He wasn't okay," I said, "so I took him away to treat him."

"Bring him back right this instant," Rosolio said. "We'll take care of him. He'll recover. What do you think would happen if all mothers took their children home? Who would win this war?"

"I didn't take him home," I said. "I didn't know what to do."

"Then where are you?"

"Not far from base," I said. "At a friend's house."

"Where?" he demanded. I gave him the exact address. "Okay, so bring him back now," he said and was about to hang up.

"We'll see, he's sleeping right now," I said. "I don't think he can take it."

The line was silent. "Listen, Abigail," Rosolio whispered into the phone, "he isn't just any other soldier. This'll cause an enormous scandal. This isn't your private business."

"What do you mean, he isn't just any other soldier?" I asked. I was standing out in the yard and the sun was diving west. I couldn't stop it. Our deadline was approaching with terrifying speed.

"Oh, Abigail," he sighed, "you can't keep this kind of thing a secret. Were you born yesterday? Everyone in the brigade knows who his father is, and soon enough the entire country will know."

"How do they know? Who told them? Even Shauli doesn't know. What are you talking about?"

"I'm not too far away," Rosolio said, "stay where you are. I'll come by to speak to you for a few moments without my entourage. The kid has to go back. I'll convince him."

Everybody knew, he'd said. I wanted to double over with pain on the ground and never get up. I gathered the uniform, which had dried in the heat of the intense sun, and walked inside.

Mandy was standing next to the sleeping Shauli, knife in hand, and asked, "Should I do it now?"

"No!" I cried. "It's too late now, and it was an insane idea to begin with. How would he play the guitar?" I shook Shauli awake. "Get up, Shauli, it's time to get up. I cleaned your uniform. Get dressed."

All the fear in the world was in his face as he slowly rose from the sofa.

"Come on, give me your foot," I asked him. I pulled the pants up one of his legs, then the other, just like when he was a baby. How was he supposed to fight when he couldn't even put on his own clothes? After I laced up his boots, I looked into his eyes, searching them for a hint of laughter or tears, anything I could connect with.

"You don't know what I saw there," Shauli said. That was good, he was talking. "You remember one day on my way home from school I saw a cat that had been run over, his guts all spilled out, and I couldn't sleep after that? There were people like that there. You have no idea what's going on there, Mom, they didn't tell us it was going to be this way."

"I wish you didn't have to go back," I said, "but there's no choice. Your dad will be here soon to take you."

"Dad is coming?" he asked. "Okay, Mom." He wasn't surprised at all. He sat up on the sofa, tall and obedient, knees close together, waiting.

I hurried to the kitchen and quickly made him a bag of sandwiches and fruit from Mandy's orchard, which I placed in his lap.

We heard the chopper landing in the open field outside of Mandy's house, the dust clouds it kicked up spinning before our eyes. Rosolio walked in on his own, leaving his guards and assistants outside. Mandy was nowhere to be seen.

"Are you ready, Shauli?" he asked, taking a few large strides inside and resting his hand on Shauli's shoulder.

"Yes, Dad, I'm ready."

They walked outside, side by side, a young soldier and an aging soldier. I stood in the doorway and watched them walking away, Rosolio talking and Shauli nodding, until they climbed into the chopper and took off, back to the front line.

19

A FEW WEEKS after Rosolio completed his term as Chief of Staff, we met at a café at the beach. It was morning, and he was wearing civilian clothing. Only one bodyguard watched over him from a distance, and we drew no attention. His little war was all but forgotten. The politicians, he claimed, had blocked him a moment before a decisive victory, stealing away his glory. Now he wanted to get my advice about the next phase in his life. We talked leisurely. As usual, he valued my opinion. Then he asked what I'd been hearing from Shauli, who'd been traveling abroad for over a year, ever since he'd completed his service. I told him he'd been writing to me occasionally, reporting on his whereabouts, but that I didn't know much beyond that. I'd asked Shauli to send photos so that I could analyze them for clues regarding his state of mind, but he didn't send a single one. From time to time, on Fridays or holidays, I got a hold of him on the phone and we had a brief conversation. Enough, at least, to know that he was alive.

"You need to know that once I returned him to base he functioned perfectly," Rosolio said. He looked soft and extinguished without his uniform. "I asked his commanders to keep an eye on him, but there was no need. He fought just like everyone else."

I tried to get the two of them to meet after the war. I expected Rosolio to agree, but he evaded us, and wouldn't meet with Shauli even once. "Why don't you write to him?" I asked. The table was strewn with the remains of our breakfast and he was looking around for an escape route. "That would be a nice thing to do. It might help."

Rosolio mumbled something.

"What did you say?" I asked. I wasn't about to let him get away with this.

"I got your book," he said, changing the subject. "Looks very impressive. I haven't had a chance to read it yet. Someone ought to translate it, so that other countries can learn from our combat experience."

"I want you to write to Shauli," I insisted, "and offer to meet him. You've got a lot of free time now. Why don't you travel together? It'll do both of you good."

"That's impossible, Abigail," Rosolio said. "I've got a wife, I've got daughters. I can't just disappear on them. We had an agreement."

I got up, walked over to the counter, and paid the bill. Then I left the café without saying goodbye. Rosolio stayed at the table, abandoned and gray, as the bodyguard watched him from a distance, face frozen.

*

Noga and I remained friends. We met often. She'd made her way through the war with flying colors, carrying Dad's cyanide pill in her pocket, and everyone was pleased with her performance. Now she was a deputy squadron commander with a glowing future ahead of her. She was the greatest of my accomplishments.

One day, after the war, we went back to see the tattoo artist.

"Have you made up your mind, Mom?" he asked, inviting me to lie down on the bed.

"Yes," I said.

"What did you choose? A flower? A bird? A loved one's name? A child's? A good luck charm?"

"A dagger, down there." I pointed at my lower stomach, almost at the hipbone.

272

"Are you sure? That's a painful spot."

"Yes. Let it hurt," I said.

He went to work.

The wound healed, and the dagger was etched into my skin. I liked it. Noga said it was pretty and frightening.

I called Jonah, having not seen him for a long time, and invited him over.

"I have a surprise for you," I said as he undressed me, awakening anticipation in his frozen eyes. "Touch it, it's for you," I whispered as the dagger was revealed. I wanted to storm like I had back then, when we'd pulled the trigger together.

YISHAI SARID was born in Tel Aviv, Israel in 1965. He is the son of senior politician and journalist Yossi Sarid. Between 1974 and 1977, he lived with his family in the northern town of Kiryat Shmona, near the Lebanon border. Sarid was recruited to the Israeli army in 1983 and served for five years. During his service, he finished the IDF's officer school, and served as an intelligence officer. He studied law at the Hebrew University of Jerusalem. From 1994 to 1997, he worked for the government as an assistant district attorney in Tel Aviv, prosecuting criminal cases. Sarid has a master's degree in Public Administration (MPA) from the Harvard Kennedy School (1999). Nowadays he is an active lawyer and arbitrator, practicing mainly civil and administrative law. His law office is located in Tel Aviv. Alongside his legal career, Sarid writes literature, and so far he has published six novels. His novels have been translated into ten languages and have won literary prizes. Sarid is married to Dr. Racheli Sion-Sarid, a critical care pediatrician, and they have three children.

YARDENNE GREENSPAN is a writer and Hebrew translator born in Tel Aviv and based in New York. Her translations have been published by Restless Books, St. Martin's Press, Akashic Books, Syracuse University, New Vessel Press, Amazon Crossing, and Farrar, Straus and Giroux. Her translation of Yishai Sarid's novel *The Memory Monster* was selected as one of the *New York Times* 100 Notable Books of 2020. Yardenne's writing and translations have appeared in the *New Yorker*, *Haaretz*, *Guernica*, *Literary Hub*, *Blunderbuss Magazine*, *Apogee*, the *Massachusetts Review, Asymptote*, and *Words Without Borders*, among other publications. She has an MFA from Columbia University and is a regular contributor to *Ploughshares*.

RESTLESS BOOKS is an independent, nonprofit publisher devoted to championing essential voices from around the world whose stories speak to us across linguistic and cultural borders. We seek extraordinary international literature for adults and young readers that feeds our restlessness: our hunger for new perspectives, passion for other cultures and languages, and eagerness to explore beyond the confines of the familiar.

Through cultural programming, we aim to celebrate immigrant writing and bring literature to underserved communities. We believe that immigrant stories are a vital component of our cultural consciousness; they help to ensure awareness of our communities, build empathy for our neighbors, and strengthen our democracy.